A COUNTRY DOCTOR'S NOTEBOOK

MIKHAIL AFANASIEVICH BULGAKOV was born in Kiev in 1891, the son of a professor at the Kiev Theological Academy. He graduated as a doctor from Kiev University in 1916, but gave up the practice of medicine in 1920 to devote himself to literature. By 1923 he was earning a living as a freelance journalist contributing largely humorous pieces to a wide range of newspapers and trade union journals. In 1925 he completed the satirical novella *The Heart of a Dog*, which remained unpublished in the Soviet Union until 1987. This was one of many defeats he was to suffer at the hands of the censors. During 1925 and 1926 three collections of his short stories, including *Diaboliad*, were published, and serialization of his novel *The White Guard* began in *Rossiya*, although the journal was closed down following an outcry from Party-line critics before the final instalment appeared. Together with the publication of the stories in the present collection, which first appeared between 1925 and 1927 in *Krasnaya panorama* and *Meditsinsky rabotnik*, these works marked Bulgakov's last appearance in print until after Stalin's death. *The White Guard* was dramatized in 1926 at the Moscow Arts Theatre under the title *The Days of the Turbins*, but was so controversial that it was banned for years at a time. By 1930 Bulgakov had become so frustrated by the political atmosphere and the suppression of his works that he wrote to Stalin begging to be allowed to emigrate if he was not to be allowed to make his living as a writer in the USSR. Stalin telephoned him personally and offered to arrange a job for him at the Moscow Arts Theatre instead. Bulgakov wrote a number of plays and an unfinished novel, *Black Snow*, in which he satirizes Stanislavsky. In 1938, a year before contracting a fatal illness, he completed his prose masterpiece, *The Master and Margarita*. He died in 1940. In 1966-67, thanks to the persistence of his widow, the novel made a first incomplete appearance in *Moskva*, and in 1973 appeared in full. Authoritative new editions of his works are now being prepared in Moscow.

The Heart of a Dog, *The White Guard* and *The Master and Margarita* are also available as Harvill Paperbacks.

Mikhail Bulgakov

A COUNTRY
DOCTOR'S NOTEBOOK

Translated from the Russian by
Michael Glenny

COLLINS HARVILL
8 Grafton Street, London W1
1990

COLLINS HARVILL
William Collins Sons and Co Ltd
London · Glasgow · Sydney · Auckland
Toronto · Johannesburg

BRITISH LIBRARY CATALOGUING IN PUBLICATION DATA

Bulgakov, Mikhail *1891-1940*
A country doctor's notebook
I. Title
891.73'42 [F]

ISBN 0-00-271064-1

First published in Great Britain by Collins & Harvill Press 1975
This paperback edition first published by Collins Harvill 1990

Translation © Michael Glenny 1975

Printed and bound in Great Britain by
William Collins Sons and Co Ltd, Glasgow

CONTENTS

INTRODUCTION

There have been several doctor-writers, Russian and English, in recent times – Chekhov, Somerset Maugham and A. J. Cronin are perhaps three of the best known – and with this collection of stories Mikhail Bulgakov is revealed as another writer who gained his earliest and perhaps his deepest insights into human nature through the practice of medicine.

Born in 1891, Mikhail Bulgakov was the eldest of the six children of a professor at Kiev Theological Academy. He studied at Kiev University and qualified in medicine in 1916. After eighteen strenuous months in general practice (the subject-matter of most of this book) he decided to specialise, and set up in Kiev as a venereologist. Another eighteen months or so later, the upheavals of the Civil War caused Bulgakov to move to the Caucasus, where he resolved to give up medicine in favour of writing. One of his brothers, Nikolai Bulgakov, was also a doctor, but whereas Mikhail practised only for a few years, stayed in Russia and died there, Nikolai emigrated to France after the revolution and made a distinguished career in Paris as a cardiologist.

By 1916, despite heavy losses from two years of fighting, the Russian army was only capable of absorbing a marginal increase in manpower. This factor, together with the strain placed on civilian medical resources by mobilisation, meant that Bulgakov and many of his fellow graduates of that year were not conscripted as army doctors. Without doing the normal hospital internship on qualifying, they were instead drafted to local government clinics and country hospitals all over Russia. It is perhaps not generally realised that pre-revolutionary Russia possessed a very creditable rural medical service, financed and managed by the provincial government authorities or *Zemstvos*. These were elective bodies, of which the nearest British equivalents are perhaps the County Councils, and they were responsible for such matters as education, roads and public health.

Since there were too few incentives or facilities for general practitioners to function outside the larger towns, the medical care of the peasantry in the outlying countryside was chiefly undertaken by the *Zemstvo*, through a network of polyclinics or small one-doctor hospitals of about forty beds. The standard of this service varied from province to province according to the relative wealth, zeal and efficiency of the different *Zemstvos*. Bulgakov served his medical apprenticeship near the village of Nikolskoye in the province or *guberniya* of Smolensk, one of the north-western regions of European Russia, and to judge by his description of the facilities and equipment available to him, the medical services of this *Zemstvo* were among the best.

Even so, it is very clear from these stories that as a means of initiation into medicine, Bulgakov's assignment to this remote country practice was much like learning to swim by being thrown into the deep end of the pool. Nowadays it can only be in some of the remoter parts of the 'third world' that totally inexperienced young doctors find themselves 'thirty-two miles from the nearest electric light', entirely cut off from the outside world for long spells, or obliged to keep a pack of wolves at bay with a pistol while driving back from a night call. Perhaps most demoralising for a nervous beginner were the primitive communications: carts or sleighs the only transport, roads that were poor at the best of times and often impassable in the springtime thaw or the winter blizzards, erratic mails or none for weeks on end and above all – no telephone. The effects of this isolation and confinement on anyone of less than robust and balanced temperament is grimly illustrated in the story called 'Morphine'.

For Bulgakov, however, the greatest underlying source of unease, amounting at times to despair, was something less tangible though very real to him, since it occurs as an ever-present refrain throughout these stories. This was the sense of being a lone soldier of reason and enlightenment pitted against the vast, dark, ocean-like mass of peasant ignorance and super-stition. Again and again Bulgakov stresses what it meant to experience in physical reality the moral anomaly which for a century and more before the revolution had caused such agony to the liberal, educated élite of Russia: that intolerable dis-crepancy between the advanced civilisation and culture enjoyed by a small minority and the fearsome, pre-literate, mediaeval world of the peasantry. Although his patients are his con-temporaries and fellow citizens of what purports to be a modern state, Bulgakov is constantly haunted by an awareness that in dealing with them he is actually at the point of contact between two cultures which are about five hundred years apart in time. It is books like this which make one appreciate the tremendous achievements of the Soviet education programme since 1917.

It will not escape the reader's notice that much of Bulgakov's narrative dwells on night, winter, blizzards and gales. This is not just a literary device to heighten the sense of drama, urgency and danger: it expresses the author's profound feeling that in the rural Russia of his early career, a doctor was literally someone fighting an elemental force. The dominant, recurrent image in his stories is that of light and dark: the light over the gateway to his little hospital, the welcoming green-shaded lamp in his study, the single light burning in an otherwise darkened, storm-swept building. These brave pinpoints of light – the light of reason – are always contrasted with the vast, malevolent, surrounding darkness which threatens to engulf them yet never succeeds in putting them out.

Despite this background intimation of an almost mythic conflict between enlightenment and unreason, Bulgakov's writing in *A Country Doctor's Notebook* is thoroughly down-to-earth, realistic, and far removed from the grotesque fantasy that was the distinctive style of much of his other work in the mid-twenties. This contrast is so marked that it is hard to credit 'Dr Bulgakov' as being also the author of such fierce, surrealistic satire as *The Heart of a Dog* and the diablerie of *The Master and Margarita*. These date from Bulgakov's richly productive period of 1924–1927, when the publication of his first novel, *The White Guard*, and the overnight success of its subsequent stage version, *The Days of the Turbins*, were making it possible for him to give up hack journalism for a living and turn to full-time writing for the theatre. Yet at the same time Bulgakov would, as it were, regularly lay aside the sardonic *persona* of the satirist and put on again the white coat he had finally doffed some five or six years earlier and would recreate, with keen, fresh observation and gentle self-deprecating humour, the agonies and triumphs of a medical novice pitched into a job of terrifying responsibility.

The result was a collection of partly-fictional, partly-auto-biographical stories; between 1925 and 1927 they were published serially in two monthlies, *Krasnaya panorama* and *Meditsinsky rabotnik*, the former being a magazine with a general readership, the latter meant particularly for the medical profession. When the series was finished, Bulgakov intended to collate and edit its parts for publication as a separate book to be entitled *The Notes of a Young Doctor* (*Zapiski yunovo vracha*). But this plan was never realised, and the stories passed into oblivion along with the magazines in which they had appeared. Almost forty years later and long after Bulgakov's death (he died in 1940), they were unearthed and some of them published in the magazine *Ogonyok*. This was followed in 1966 by the appearance of six of these stories in an edition of Bulgakov's *Collected Prose*. It is this book which has provided the text of two-thirds of the present collection; the remaining three stories – 'The Murderer', 'Morphine' and 'The Speckled Rash' – were translated from photostats of copies of *Meditsinsky rabotnik* found in Moscow archives. For kindly making the latter available to me I am greatly indebted to Mr Peter Doyle of the University of Manchester. My gratitude for her assistance with the texts is due to Miss K. Costello. I also wish to express particular thanks to the two medical men, Dr Hope St John Brooks and Dr Robert Salo, who have so kindly cast their keen professional eyes over the translation and corrected the terminology of a mere layman.

MICHAEL GLENNY

The Embroidered Towel

If you have never driven over country roads it is useless for me to tell you about it; you wouldn't understand anyway. But if you have, I would rather not remind you of it.

To cut a long story short, my driver and I spent exactly twenty-four hours covering the thirty-two miles which separate the district town of Grachyovka from Muryovo hospital. Indeed so nearly exactly twenty-four hours that it was uncanny: at 2 p.m. on 16 September 1916 we were at the last corn-chandler's store on the outskirts of the remarkable town of Grachyovka, and at five past two on 17 September of that same unforgettable year 1916, I was in the Muryovo hospital yard, standing on trampled, withered grass, flattened by the September rain. My legs were ossified with cold, so much so that as I stood there bemused, I mentally leafed through the textbook pages in an inane attempt to remember whether there was such a complaint as ossification of the muscles or whether it was an illness I had dreamed up while asleep the night before in the village of Grabilovka. What the devil was it in Latin? Every single muscle ached unbearably, like toothache. There is nothing I can say about my toes – they lay immobile in my boots, as rigid as wooden stumps. I confess that in a burst of cowardice I pronounced a whispered curse on the medical profession and on the application form I had handed in five years earlier to the rector of the university. All the time a fine rain was drizzling down as through a sieve. My coat had swelled like a sponge. I vainly tried to grasp my suitcase with the fingers of my right hand, but in the end spat on the wet grass in disgust. My fingers were incapable of gripping anything. It was then, stuffed as I was with all sorts of knowledge from fascinating medical books, that I suddenly remembered the name of the illness – palsy. 'Paralysis', I said to myself in despair, God knows why.

'Your roads take some getting used to,' I muttered through stony, blue lips, staring resentfully at the driver, although the state of the road was hardly his fault.

'Ah, comrade doctor,' he answered, with lips equally stiff under their fair moustache, 'I've been driving fifteen years and I still can't get used to them.'

I shuddered and glanced round miserably at the peeling, white, two-storey hospital building, at the bare log walls of my assistant's house, and at my own future residence, a neat, two-storey house with mysterious windows blank as gravestones. I gave a long sigh. Suddenly instead of Latin words a faraway memory flashed through my head, a sweet phrase which a lusty tenor in blue stockings sang in my numbed and shaken head: *Salut, demeure chaste et pure* . . . Farewell, farewell, it will be a long time before I see you again, oh golden-red Bolshoi Theatre, Moscow, shop windows . . . ah, farewell.

'Next time, I'll wear a sheepskin coat,' I said to myself in angry desperation, tugging at the suitcase by its straps with my inflexible hands. 'I'll . . . though next time it'll be mid-October, I'll have to wear two sheepskin coats. I certainly shan't be going to Grachyovka for a month yet. Just think . . . I actually had to put up for the night en route! When we had only driven fifteen miles and it was as black as the tomb . . . it was night . . . we had to stop in Grabilovka, a school teacher put us up. This morning we set off at seven in the morning, and here we are . . . God, it's been slower driving here than if we'd come on foot. One wheel got stuck in a ditch, the other swung up into the air, my case fell on to my feet with a crash, we slithered from side to side, lurching forward one moment, backward the next. And all the time a fine rain drizzling down and my bones turning to ice. Who'd believe you can freeze as easily in the middle of a grey, miserable September as in the depth of winter? Ah well, it seems you can. And as you die a slow death there's nothing to look at except the same endless monotony. On the right the bare, undulating fields and on the left a stunted copse, flanked by five or six grey, dilapidated shacks. Not a living soul in them, it seems, and not a sound to be heard.'

In the end the suitcase yielded. The driver lay on his

stomach and shoved it down on top of me. I tried to catch it by the strap but my hand refused to perform and the beastly thing, crammed with books and all sorts of rubbish, flopped down on to the grass, crashing against my legs.

'Oh Lor . . .' the driver began fearfully, but I did not complain. My legs were no more sensitive than two sticks of wood.

'Hey, anybody at home? Hey!' the driver cried out and flapped his arms like a rooster flapping its wings. 'Hey, I've brought the doctor!'

At once faces appeared, pressed against the dark windows of the assistant's house. A door banged and I saw a man hobbling towards me in a ragged coat and worn old boots. He hurriedly and respectfully doffed his cap, ran up and stopped two paces short of me, then smiling somewhat bashfully he welcomed me in a hoarse voice:

'Good day, comrade doctor.'

'And who might you be?' I asked.

'I'm Yegorich,' he introduced himself, 'the watchman here. We've been expecting you.'

Without wasting a moment he grabbed the suitcase, swung it over his shoulder and carried it in. I limped after him, trying unsuccessfully to thrust my hand into my trouser pocket to get out my purse.

Man's basic needs are few. The first of them is fire. Back in Moscow, when I found out that I was to go to remote Muryovo, I had promised myself that I would behave in a dignified manner. My youthful appearance made life intolerable for me in those early days. I always made a point of introducing myself as 'Doctor So-and-So', and inevitably people raised their eyebrows and said:

'Really? I thought you were still a student.'

'No. I'm qualified,' I would answer sullenly, thinking: 'I must start wearing spectacles, that's what I must do.' But there was no point in this, as I had perfectly good vision, my eyes as yet unclouded by experience. Unable to wear glasses as a defence against those invariable, affectionately indulgent smiles, I tried to develop a special manner designed to induce respect. I tried to talk evenly and gravely, to repress impulsive movements as far as possible, to walk and not run as twenty-four-year-olds do who have just left university. Looking back, I now realise that the attempt did not come off at all.

At the moment in question I disobeyed my unwritten code of behaviour. I sat hunched up in front of the fire with my shoes off, not in the study but in the kitchen, like a fire-worshipper, fervently and passionately drawn to the birch logs blazing in the stove. On my left stood an upturned tub with my boots lying on top of it, next to them a plucked cockerel with a bloodstained neck, and its many-coloured feathers lying in a heap beside it. While still stiff with the cold, I had somehow managed to perform a whole set of vital actions. I had confirmed Yegorich's wife, the sharp-nosed Aksinya, in her position as my cook. As a result of this she had slaughtered the cockerel and I was to eat it. I had been introduced to everyone in turn. My *feldsher** was called Demyan Lukich, the midwives were Pelagea Ivanovna and Anna Nikolaevna. I had been shown round the hospital and was left in no doubt whatever that it was generously equipped. With equal certainty I was forced to admit (inwardly, of course) that I had no idea what very many of these shiny, unsullied instruments were for. Not only had I never held them in my hands, but to tell the truth I had never even seen them.

'Hm,' I mumbled significantly, 'must say you have an excellent set of instruments. Hm . . .'

'Oh sir,' Demyan Lukich remarked sweetly, 'this is all thanks to your predecessor Leopold Leopoldovich. You see, he used to operate from dawn till dusk.'

I was instantly covered with cold sweat and stared glumly at the gleaming cupboards.

We then went round the empty wards and I satisfied myself that they could easily hold forty patients.

'Leopold Leopoldovich sometimes had fifty in here,' Demyan Lukich said consolingly, and Anna Nikolaevna, a woman with a diadem of grey hair, chose to say:

'Doctor, you look so young, so very young . . . it's simply amazing. You look like a student.'

'Oh, hell,' I said to myself, 'really, you'd think they were doing it on purpose!'

Through clenched teeth I grunted:

'Hm . . . no, well, I . . . yes, rather young looking . . .'

After that we went down to the pharmacy and a glance was enough to tell me that it was supplied with every conceivable medicine. Its two sombre rooms smelled strongly of herbs and its

*A partly-qualified medical assistant.

shelves were filled with an endless variety of preparations. There were even foreign patent medicines, which, need I add, I had never heard of.

'Leopold Leopoldovich ordered these,' Pelagea Ivanovna reported proudly.

'This Leopold was nothing short of a genius,' I thought and was filled with respect for the mysterious Leopold who had left the quiet little village of Muryovo behind him.

Besides fire, man also needs to find his bearings. I had long since eaten the cockerel, Yegorich had stuffed my mattress with straw and covered it with a sheet, and a light was burning in my study. Spellbound, I sat and stared at the legendary Leopold's third great achievement: the book-case was crammed with books. I counted roughly thirty volumes of surgery manuals in Russian and German. And the books on therapeutics! The beautiful leather-bound anatomical atlases!

Evening drew on and I started to find my bearings.

'It's not my fault,' I repeated to myself stubbornly and unhappily. 'I've got my degree and a first class one at that. Didn't I warn them back in town that I wanted to start off as a junior partner in a practice? But no, they just smiled and said, "You'll get your bearings." So now I've got to find my bearings. Suppose they bring me a hernia? Just tell me how I'll find my bearings with that? And more to the point, what will a hernia patient feel like when I get my hands on him? Will he find his bearings in the next world?' The thought made my blood run cold.

'What about peritonitis? Oh no! Or croup, that country children get? When is tracheotomy indicated? Even if it doesn't need tracheotomy I shall be pretty much at sea . . . What about . . . what about . . . deliveries! I forgot about deliveries! Incorrect positions. What on earth will I do? What a fool I was! I should have refused this job. I really should. They should have found themselves another Leopold.'

Miserable, I paced up and down the twilit study. When I came up to the lamp I caught sight of the reflection of my pale face and of the light of the lamp in the window set against the boundless darkness of the fields.

'I'm like Dmitry the Pretender – nothing but a sham,' I thought stupidly and sat down at the table again.

I spent about two lonely hours of self-torment and only stopped when my nerves could no longer bear the horrors I had summoned up. Then I started to calm down and even to work out a plan of action.

'Let's see now . . . they tell me admissions are almost nil at the moment. They're braking flax in the villages, the roads are impassable . . .'

'That's just when they will bring you a hernia,' thundered a harsh voice in my mind, 'because a man with a cold won't make the effort over impassable roads but rest assured they'll bring you a hernia, my dear doctor.'

There was something in what the voice said. I shuddered.

'Be quiet,' I said to it. 'It won't necessarily be a hernia. Stop being so neurotic. You can't back out once you've begun.'

'You said it!' the voice answered spitefully.

'All right then . . . I won't take a step without my reference book . . . If I have to prescribe something I can think it over while I wash my hands and the reference book will be lying open on top of the patients' register. I shall make out wholesome but simple prescriptions, say, sodium salicylate, 0.5 grammes in powder form three times a day.'

'You might as well prescribe baking soda! Why don't you just prescribe soda?' the voice was blatantly making fun of me.

'What's soda got to do with it? I'll also prescribe an infusion of ipecacuanha, 180 c.c. Or 200 c.c. if you don't mind.'

And although no one was asking for ipecacuanha as I sat there alone by the lamp, I sheepishly turned the pages in the pharmacopoeia and checked ipecacuanha; meanwhile I automatically read in passing that there was a certain substance called 'Insipin' which is none other than 'ethereal sulphate of quinine-diglycolic acid'. Apparently it doesn't taste of quinine! What is it for? And how is it prescribed? What is it, a powder? To hell with it!

'That's all very well, but what are you going to do about a hernia?' The voice of Fear continued to pester me.

'I'll put them into a bath,' I defended myself in exasperation, 'and try to reduce it.'

'What if it's a strangulated one, old boy? Baths won't be much use then, will they! A strangulated hernia!' Fear chanted in a demoniac voice, 'You'll have to cut it out . . . !'

I gave in and all but burst into tears. I sent out a prayer to the darkness outside the window: please, anything but not a strangulated hernia.

Weariness then crooned:

'Go to bed, unhappy physician. Sleep on it. Calm down and stop being neurotic. Look how still the dark is outside the window, the fields are cold and sleeping, there is no hernia. You can think about it in the morning. You'll settle down . . . Sleep . . . drop that book of diagrams, you won't make head or tail of it anyway . . . hernial orifice . . .'

I don't remember him arriving. I only remember the bolt grating in the door, a shriek from Aksinya and a cart creaking out in the yard.

He was hatless, his sheepskin coat unbuttoned, his beard was dishevelled and there was a mad look in his eyes.

He crossed himself, fell on his knees and banged his forehead against the floor. This to me!

'I'm a lost man,' I thought wretchedly.

'Now, now – what's the matter?' I muttered and pulled at his grey sleeve.

His face twisted and he started mumbling a breathless and incoherent answer:

'Oh doctor, sir . . . sir . . . she's all I've got, she's all I've got, she's all I've got,' he burst out suddenly in a voice so young-sounding and powerful that the lampshade trembled. 'Oh, sir, oh . . .' He wrung his hands in misery and started knocking his forehead against the floorboards as if trying to smash them. 'Why? Why am I being punished? What have I done to deserve God's anger?'

'What is it? What's happened?' I cried out, feeling the blood draining from my face.

He jumped to his feet, rushed towards me and whispered:

'Anything you want, doctor, sir . . . I'll give you money, take as much money as you want. As much as you want. We'll pay you in food if you like. Only don't let her die. Don't let her die. Even if she's to be a cripple, I don't mind. I don't mind!' He shouted to the ceiling. 'I've got enough to feed her, I can manage.'

I could see Aksinya's pale face in the black rectangle of the door. I was overcome with anguish.

'Well, what is it? Speak!' I cried irritably.

He stopped. His eyes went blank and he whispered, as if telling me a secret:

'She fell into the brake.'

'Brake . . . brake? What's that?'
'Flax, they were braking flax, doctor,' Aksinya whispered in explanation, 'you know, brake, flax braking . . .'
'Here's a fine beginning. This is it. Oh why did I ever come?' I said to myself in horror.
'Who?'
'My daughter,' he answered in a whisper, and then shouted, 'Help me!' Once again he threw himself to the floor and his hair, cut like a mop in peasant fashion, fell into his eyes.

The pressure-lamp with its lopsided tin shade burned with hot beams of light. She lay on the operating table, on white, fresh-smelling oilcloth and when I saw her all thoughts of hernia vanished from my mind.
Her fair, almost reddish hair hung down from the table in a matted clump. She had a gigantic plait which reached to the floor.
Her calico skirt was torn and stained with blood in various shades from brown to oily scarlet. The light of the kerosene lamp was a lively yellow in comparison with her paper-white face, and her nose was beginning to sharpen. On her white face, motionless as a plaster cast, a truly rare beauty was fading away before my eyes. Seldom in life does one see such a face.
The operating theatre was completely silent for about ten seconds, but from behind the closed doors came the muffled sounds of someone shouting and banging his head over and over again.
'Gone out of his mind,' I thought. 'The nurses must be seeing to him. Why is she so beautiful? Though he does have good bone structure; the mother must have been a beautiful woman. He's a widower. . . .'
'Is he a widower?' I whispered automatically.
'Yes, he is,' Pelagea Ivanovna answered quietly.
Then Demyan Lukich, almost as if in anger, ripped the skirt from hem to waist, baring her instantly. I looked, and what I saw was even worse than I had expected. Strictly speaking there was no left leg. From the smashed knee down there were just bloody shreds, battered red flesh and splinters of white bone protruding in all directions. The right leg was fractured at the shin so that the tips of both bones had punctured the skin

and her foot lay lifelessly on its side, as though disconnected.
'Yes . . .' the *feldsher* pronounced softly and that was all he
said.

Thereupon I regained my wits and started feeling her pulse.
Her cold wrist registered nothing. Only after a few seconds did I
detect a barely perceptible, irregular ripple. It passed and was
followed by a pause during which I had time to glance at her
white lips and nostrils, which were turning blue. I already felt like
saying 'It's all over', but fortunately controlled myself . . . there
was another hint of a beat.

'The end of a mangled human being,' I said to myself. 'There's
really nothing more to be done.'

But suddenly I said sternly, in a voice that I did not recognise:
'Camphor.'

Anna Nikolaevna bent over to my ear and whispered:

'What for, doctor? Don't torture her. What's the point of
smashing her up any more? She'll die any minute now . . . you
won't save her.'

I gave her an angry look and said:

'I asked for camphor . . .' in such a way that she flushed,
marched resentfully to the little table and broke an ampoule.
The *feldsher* obviously did not approve of the camphor either.
Nonetheless he deftly and swiftly took hold of a syringe and the
yellow oil went under the skin of her shoulder.

'Die. Die quickly,' I said to myself. 'Die. Otherwise what am I
to do with you?'

'She'll die now,' whispered the *feldsher* as if guessing my
thoughts. He glanced meaningfully at the sheet but apparently
changed his mind. It seemed a pity to stain it with blood. But a
few seconds later he had to cover her. She lay like a corpse, but
did not die. Suddenly my head became quite clear, as if I were
standing under the glass roof of the anatomy theatre in that
faraway medical school.

'Camphor again,' I said hoarsely.

And once again the *feldsher* obediently injected the oil.

'Is she really not going to die?' I thought in despair. 'Will I
really have to . . .'

Everything lit up in my mind and I suddenly became aware
without any textbooks, without any advice or help (and with
unshakeable conviction), that now, for the first time in my life I
had to perform an amputation on a dying person. And that that

person would die under the knife. She was bound to die under the knife; after all, there was no blood left in her body. It had all drained out through her shattered legs over six miles and there was not even a sign that she was conscious. She was silent. Oh, why didn't she die? What would her maddened father say to me?

'Prepare for an amputation,' I said to the assistant in a voice that was not my own.

The midwife gave me a fierce look but the *feldsher* showed a spark of sympathy in his eyes and began busying himself with the instruments. A primus-stove started to roar.

A quarter of an hour passed. I raised her cold eyelid and looked with superstitious fear at the expiring eye. It told me nothing. How could a semi-corpse stay alive? Drops of sweat ran uncontrollably down my forehead from under my white cap and Pelagea wiped away the salt sweat with gauze. What remained of the blood in the girl's veins was now diluted with caffeine. Ought it to have been injected or not? Anna Nikolaevna was gently massaging the swellings caused by the saline solution. And the girl lived on.

I picked up the knife, trying to imitate the man I had once in my life seen perform an amputation, at university. I entreated fate not to let her die at least in the next half hour. 'Let her die in the ward, when I've finished the operation . . .'

I had only common sense to rely on, and it was stimulated into action by the extraordinary situation. Like an experienced butcher, I made a neat circular incision in her thigh with the razor-sharp knife and the skin parted without exuding the smallest drop of blood. 'What will I do if the vessels start bleeding?' I thought, and without turning my head glanced at the row of forceps. I cut through a huge piece of female flesh together with one of the vessels – it looked like a little whitish pipe – but not a drop of blood emerged from it. I stopped it up with a pair of forceps and proceeded, clamping on forceps wherever I suspected the existence of a vessel. 'Arteria . . . arteria . . . what the devil is it called?' The operating theatre had begun to take on a thoroughly professional look. The forceps were hanging in clusters. My assistants drew them back with gauze, retracting the flesh, and I started sawing the round bone with a gleaming, fine-toothed saw. 'Why isn't she dying? It's astonishing . . . God, how people cling to life!'

The bone fell away. Demyan Lukich was left with what had been a girl's leg in his hands. Shreds of flesh and bone. This was all discarded and there remained on the table a young girl shortened, as it were, by a third, with a stump splayed out to one side. 'Just a little bit more . . . Please don't die,' I wished ardently, 'keep going till they take you to the ward, let me come out of this frightful episode with some credit.'

They tied the ligatures and then, knees knocking, I started sewing up the skin with widely-spaced stitches. Suddenly I stopped, brought to my senses by an inspired thought: I left a gap for drainage in which I inserted a gauze wick. My eyes were dimmed with sweat. I felt as if I were in a steam bath.

I heaved a sigh of relief. I looked wearily at the stump and at her waxen face and asked:

'Is she alive?'

'Yes, she's alive,' came the immediate and almost soundless echo as the *feldsher* and Anna Nikolaevna replied in unison.

'She'll last perhaps another minute or so,' the *feldsher* mouthed voicelessly into my ear. Then he hesitated and suggested tentatively:

'Perhaps you needn't touch the other leg, doctor. We could just bandage it, you know . . . otherwise she won't last till the ward . . . all right? Better if she doesn't die in the theatre.'

'Let's have the plaster,' I uttered hoarsely, urged on by some unknown force.

The floor was covered in white blobs of gypsum. We were all bathed in sweat. The body lay lifeless. Its right leg was encased in plaster and the shin showed through where in another inspired moment I had left a window to coincide with the fracture.

'She's alive,' the assistant breathed in surprise.

Then we started lifting her and an enormous cavity could be seen under the sheet – we had left a third of her body on the operating table.

Shadows flitted down the passage, nurses darted to and fro and I saw a dishevelled male figure shuffle past along the wall and let out a muffled howl. But he was led away. Silence fell.

In the operating room I washed off the blood which had stained my arms up to the elbow.

'I suppose you've done a lot of amputations, doctor?' Anna Nikolaevna asked suddenly. 'That was very good, no worse than Leopold.'

She invariably pronounced the name 'Leopold' as if she were talking about the dean of a medical school.

I glanced suspiciously at their faces and saw respect and astonishment in all of them, including Demyan Lukich and Pelagea Ivanovna.

'Hm, well, the fact is I've done only two . . .'

Why did I lie? I cannot understand it to this day.

The hospital was utterly silent.

'When she dies, be sure to send for me,' I told the *feldsher* in an undertone, and for some reason instead of just answering 'All right,' he said deferentially:

'Very good, sir.'

A few minutes later I was standing beside the green-shaded lamp in the study of the doctor's quarters. There was not a sound to be heard.

A pale face was reflected in the pitch-dark window.

'No, I don't look like Dmitry the Pretender, and, do you know, I seem to have aged, there's a furrow between my eyebrows . . . right now there'll be a knock . . . and they'll say, "She's dead".

'Yes, I'll go and have a last look, any minute now there'll be a knock . . .'

There was a knock at the door. It was two and a half months later. One of the first bright days of winter was shining through the window.

He came in; only then did I really look at him. Yes, he definitely had good features. Forty-five years old. Sparkling eyes.

Then a rustling sound. A young girl of enchanting beauty came bounding in on crutches; she had only one leg and was dressed in a very wide skirt with a red border at the hem.

She looked at me and her cheeks flushed pink.

'In Moscow . . . in Moscow,' I said and started writing down an address, 'they'll fix you up with a prosthesis – an artificial leg.'

'Kiss his hand,' the father suddenly commanded her.

I was so confused that I kissed her on the nose instead of the lips.

Then, hanging on her crutches, she undid a bundle and out fell a snow-white towel artlessly embroidered with a red cockerel. So that was what she'd been hiding under her pillow when I did my rounds in the ward! And indeed I remembered seeing some thread on her bedside table.

'I can't accept it,' I said sternly, and even shook my head. But she gave me such a look that I took it.

It hung in my bedroom in Muryovo and then went with me on my travels. In the end it grew threadbare, faded, wore out and disappeared just as memories fade and disappear.

The Steel Windpipe

So I was alone, surrounded by November gloom and whirling snow; the house was smothered in it and there was a moaning in the chimneys. I had spent all twenty-four years of my life in a huge city and thought that blizzards only howled in novels. It appeared that they howled in real life. The evenings here are unusually long, and I fell to daydreaming, staring at the reflection on the window of the lamp with its dark green shade. I dreamed of the nearest town, thirty-two miles away. I longed to leave my country clinic and go there. They had electricity, and there were four doctors whom I could consult. At all events it would be less frightening than this place. But there was no chance of running away, and at times I realised that it would be cowardly. It was for precisely this, after all, that I had been studying medicine.

'Yes, but suppose they bring me a woman in labour and there are complications? Or, say, a patient with a strangulated hernia? What shall I do then? Kindly tell me that. Forty-eight days ago I qualified "with distinction"; but distinction is one thing and hernia is another. Once I watched a professor operating on a strangulated hernia. He did it, while I sat in the amphitheatre. And I only just managed to survive . . .'

More than once I broke out in a cold sweat down my spine at the thought of hernia. Every evening, as I drank my tea, I would sit in the same attitude: by my left hand lay all the manuals on obstetrical surgery, on top of them the small edition of Döderlein. To my right were ten different illustrated volumes on operative surgery. I groaned, smoked and drank cold tea without milk.

Once I fell asleep. I remember that night perfectly – it was 29 November, and I was woken by someone banging on the door. Five minutes later I was pulling on my trousers, my eyes glued imploringly to those sacred books on operative surgery. I could hear the creaking of sleigh-runners in the yard – my ears had become unusually sensitive. The case turned out to be, if anything, even more terrifying than a hernia or a transverse foetus. At eleven o'clock that night a little girl was brought to the Muryovo hospital. The nurse said tonelessly to me:

'The little girl's weak, she's dying . . . Would you come over to the hospital, please, doctor . . .'

I remember crossing the yard towards the hospital porch, mesmerised by the flickering light of a kerosene lamp. The lights were on in the surgery, and all my assistants were waiting for me, already dressed in their overalls: the *feldsher* Demyan Lukich, young but very capable, and two experienced midwives, Anna Nikolaevna and Pelagea Ivanovna. Only twenty-four years old, having qualified a mere two months ago, I had been placed in charge of the Muryovo hospital.

The *feldsher* solemnly flung open the door and the mother came in – or rather she seemed to fly in, slithering on her ice-covered felt boots, unmelted snow still on her shawl. In her arms she carried a bundle, from which came a steady hissing, whistling sound. The mother's face was contorted with noiseless weeping. When she had thrown off her sheepskin coat and shawl and unwrapped the bundle, I saw a little girl of about three years old. For a while the sight of her made me forget operative surgery, my loneliness, the load of useless knowledge acquired at university: it was all completely effaced by the beauty of this baby girl. What can I liken her to? You only see children like that on chocolate boxes – hair curling naturally into big ringlets the colour of ripe rye, enormous dark blue eyes, doll-like cheeks. They used to draw angels like that. But in the depths of her eyes was a strange cloudiness and I recognised it as terror – the child could not breathe. 'She'll be dead in an hour,' I thought with absolute certainty, feeling a sharp twinge of pity for the child.

Her throat was contracting into hollows with each breath, her veins were swollen and her face was turning from pink to a pale lilac. I immediately realised what this colouring meant. I made my first diagnosis, which was not only correct but, more important, was given at the same moment as the midwives' with all their experience: 'The little girl has diphtherial croup. Her throat is already choked with membrane and soon it will be blocked completely.'

'How long has she been ill?' I asked, breaking the tense silence of my assistants.

'Five days now,' the mother answered, staring hard at me with dry eyes.

'Diphtheria,' I said to the *feldsher* through clenched teeth, and turned to the mother:

'Why have you left it so long?'

At that moment I heard a tearful voice behind me:

'Five days, sir, five days!'

I turned round and saw that a round-faced old woman had silently come in. 'I wish these old women didn't exist,' I thought to myself. With an aching presentiment of trouble I said:

'Quiet, woman, you're only in the way,' and repeated to the mother: 'Why have you left it so long? Five days? Hmm?'

Suddenly with an automatic movement the mother handed the little girl to the grandmother and sank to her knees in front of me.

'Give her some medicine,' she said and banged her forehead on the floor. 'I'll kill myself if she dies.'

'Get up at once,' I replied, 'or I won't even talk to you.'

The mother stood up quickly with a rustle of her wide skirt, took the baby from the grandmother and started rocking it. The old woman turned to the doorpost and began praying, while the little girl continued to breathe with a snake-like hiss. The *feldsher* said:

'That's what they're all like. These people!' And he gave a twitch of his moustache.

'Does that mean she's going to die?' the mother asked, staring at me with what looked like black fury.

'Yes, she'll die,' I said quietly and firmly.

The grandmother picked up the hem of her skirt and wiped her eyes. The mother shouted in an ugly voice:

'Give her something! Help her! Give her some medicine!'

I could see what was in store for me and remained firm.

'What medicine can I give her? Go on, you tell me. The little girl is suffocating, her throat is already blocked up. For five days you kept her ten miles away from me. Now what do you want me to do?'

'You're the one who's supposed to know,' the old woman

whined by my left shoulder in an affected voice which made me immediately detest her.

'Shut up!' I said to her. I turned to the *feldsher* and ordered the little girl to be taken away. The mother handed her to the midwife and the child started to struggle, evidently trying to cry, but her voice could no longer make itself heard. The mother made a protective move towards her, but we kept her away and I managed to look into the little girl's throat by the light of the pressure-lamp. I had never seen diphtheria before except for mild, forgettable cases. Her throat was full of ragged, pulsating, white substance. The little girl suddenly breathed out and spat in my face, but I was so absorbed that I did not flinch.

'Well now,' I said, astonished at my own calm. 'This is the situation: it's late, and the little girl is dying. Nothing will help her except one thing – an operation.'

I was appalled, wondering why I had said this, but I could not help saying it. The thought flashed through my mind: 'What if she agrees to it?'

'How do you mean?' the mother asked.

'I'll have to cut open her throat near the bottom of her neck and put in a silver pipe so that she can breathe, and then maybe we can save her,' I explained.

The mother looked at me as if I was mad and shielded the little girl from me with her arms, while the old woman started muttering again:

'The idea! Don't you let them cut her open! What – cut her throat?'

'Go away, old woman,' I said to her with hatred. 'Inject the camphor!' I ordered the *feldsher*.

The mother refused to hand over the little girl when she saw the syringe, but we explained to her that there was nothing terrible about it.

'Perhaps that will cure her?' she asked.

'No, it won't cure her at all.'

Then the mother burst into tears.

'Stop it,' I said. I took out my watch, and added: 'I'm giving you five minutes to think it over. If you don't agree in five minutes, I shall refuse to do it.'

'I don't agree!' the mother said sharply.

'No, we won't agree to it,' the grandmother put in.

'It's up to you,' I said in a hollow voice, and thought: 'Well, that's that. It makes it easier for me. I've said my piece and given them a chance. Look how dumbfounded the midwives are. They've refused and I'm saved.' No sooner had I thought this than some other being spoke for me in a voice that was not mine:

'Look, have you gone mad? What do you mean by not agreeing? You're condemning the baby to death. You must consent. Have you no pity?'

'No!' the mother shouted once more.

I thought to myself: 'What am I doing? I shall only kill the child.' But I said:

'Come on, come on – you've got to agree! You must! Look, her nails are already turning blue.'

'No, no!'

'All right, take them to the ward. Let them sit there.'

They were led away down the half-lit passage. I could hear the weeping of the women and the hissing of the little girl. The *feldsher* returned almost at once and said:

'They've agreed!'

I felt my blood run cold, but I said in a clear voice:

'Sterilise a scalpel, scissors, hooks and a probe at once.'

A minute later I was running across the yard, through a swirling, blinding snowstorm. I rushed to my room and, counting the minutes, grabbed a book, leafed through it and found an illustration of a tracheotomy. Everything about it was clear and simple: the throat was laid open and the knife plunged into the windpipe. I started reading the text, but could take none of it in – the words seemed to jump before my eyes. I had never seen a tracheotomy performed. 'Ah well, it's a bit late now,' I said to myself, and looked miserably at the green lamp and the clear illustration. Feeling that I had suddenly been burdened with a most fearful and difficult task, I went back to the hospital, oblivious of the snowstorm.

In the surgery a dim figure in full skirts clung to me and a voice whined:

'Oh, sir, how can you cut a little girl's throat? How can you? She's agreed to it because she's stupid. But you haven't got my permission – no you haven't. I agree to giving her medicine, but I shan't allow her throat to be cut.'

'Get this woman out!' I shouted, and added vehemently: 'You're the stupid one! Yes, you are. And she's the clever one. Anyway, nobody asked you! Get her out of here!'

A midwife took a firm hold of the old woman and pushed her out of the room.

'Ready!' the *feldsher* said suddenly.

We went into the small operating theatre; the shiny instruments, blinding lamplight and oilcloth seemed to belong to another world . . . for the last time I went out to the mother, and the little girl could scarcely be torn from her arms. She just said in a hoarse voice: 'My husband's away in town. When he comes back and finds out what I've done, he'll kill me!'

'Yes, he'll kill her,' the old woman echoed, looking at me in horror.

'Don't let them into the operating theatre!' I ordered.

So we were left in the operating theatre, my assistants, myself, and Lidka, the little girl. She sat naked and pathetic on the table and wept soundlessly. They laid her on the table, strapped her down, washed her throat and painted it with iodine. I picked up the scalpel, still wondering what on earth I was doing. It was very quiet. With the scalpel I made a vertical incision down the swollen white throat. Not one drop of blood emerged. Again I drew the knife along the white strip which protruded between the slit skin. Again not a trace of blood. Slowly, trying to remember the illustrations in my textbooks, I started to part the delicate tissues with the blunt probe. At once dark blood gushed out from the lower end of the wound, flooding it instantly and pouring down her neck. The *feldsher* started to staunch it with swabs but could not stop the flow. Calling to mind everything I had seen at university, I set about clamping the edges of the wound with forceps, but this did no good either.

I went cold and my forehead broke out in a sweat. I bitterly regretted having studied medicine and having landed myself in this wilderness. In angry desperation I jabbed the forceps haphazardly into the region of the wound, snapped them shut and the flow of blood stopped immediately. We swabbed the wound with pieces of gauze; now it faced me clean and absolutely incomprehensible. There was no windpipe anywhere to be seen. This wound of mine was quite unlike any illustration. I spent the next two or three minutes aimlessly poking about in the wound, first with the scalpel and then with the probe, searching for the windpipe. After two minutes of this, I despaired of finding it. 'This is the end,' I thought. 'Why did I ever do this? I needn't have offered to do the operation, and Lidka could have died quietly in the ward. As it is she will die with her throat slit open and I can never prove that she would have died anyway, that I couldn't have made it any worse . . .' The midwife wiped my brow in silence. 'I ought to put down my scalpel and say: I don't know what to do next.' As I thought this I pictured the mother's eyes. I picked up the knife again and made a deep, undirected slash into Lidka's neck. The tissues parted and to my surprise the windpipe appeared before me.

'Hooks!' I croaked hoarsely.

The *feldsher* handed them to me. I pierced each side with a hook and handed one of them to him. Now I could see one thing only: the greyish ringlets of the windpipe. I thrust the sharp knife into it – and froze in horror. The windpipe was coming out of the incision and the *feldsher* appeared to have taken leave of his wits: he was tearing it out. Behind me the two midwives gasped. I looked up and saw what was the matter: the *feldsher* had fainted from the oppressive heat and, still holding the hook, was tearing at the windpipe. 'It's fate,' I thought, 'everything's against me. We've certainly murdered Lidka now.' And I added grimly to myself: 'As soon as I get back to my room, I'll shoot myself.' Then the older midwife, who was evidently very experienced, pounced on the *feldsher* and tore the hook out of his hand, saying through her clenched teeth:

'Go on, doctor . . .'

The *feldsher* collapsed to the floor with a crash but we did not turn to look at him. I plunged the scalpel into the trachea and then inserted a silver tube. It slid in easily but Lidka remained motionless. The air did not flow into her windpipe as it should have done. I sighed deeply and stopped: I had done all I could. I felt like begging someone's forgiveness for having been so thoughtless as to study medicine. Silence reigned. I could see Lidka turning blue. I was just about to give up and weep, when the child suddenly gave a violent convulsion, expelled a fountain of disgusting clotted matter through the tube, and the air whistled into her windpipe. As she started to breathe, the little girl began to howl. That instant the *feldsher* got to his feet, pale and sweaty, looked at her throat in stupefied horror and helped me to sew it up.

Dazed, my vision blurred by a film of sweat, I saw the happy faces of the midwives and one of them said to me:

'You did the operation brilliantly, doctor.'

I thought she was making fun of me and glowered at her. Then the doors were opened and a gust of fresh air blew in. Lidka was carried out wrapped in a sheet and at once the mother appeared in the doorway. Her eyes had the look of a wild beast. She asked me:

'Well?'

When I heard the sound of her voice, I felt a cold sweat run down my back as I realised what it would have been like if Lidka had died on the table. But I answered her in a very calm voice:

'Don't worry, she's alive. And she'll stay alive, I hope. Only she won't be able to talk until we take the pipe out, so don't let that upset you.'

Just then the grandmother seemed to materialise from nowhere and crossed herself, bowing to the doorhandle, to me, and to the ceiling. This time I did not lose my temper with her, I turned away and ordered Lidka to be given a camphor injection and for the staff to take turns at watching her. Then I went across the yard to my quarters. I remember the green lamp burning in my study, Döderlein lying there and books scattered everywhere. I walked over to the couch fully dressed, lay down and was immediately lost to the world in a dreamless sleep.

A month passed, then another. I grew more experienced and some of the things I saw were rather more frightening than Lidka's throat, which passed out of my mind. Snow lay all around, and the size of my practice grew daily. Early in the new year, a woman came to my surgery holding by the hand a little girl wrapped in so many layers that she looked as round as a little barrel. The woman's eyes were shining. I took a good look and recognised them.

'Ah, Lidka! How are things?'

'Everything's fine.'

The mother unwound the scarves from Lidka's neck. Though she was shy and resisted I managed to raise her chin and took a look. Her pink neck was marked with a brown vertical scar crossed by two fine stitch marks.

'All's well,' I said. 'You needn't come any more.'

'Thank you, doctor, thank you,' the mother said, and turned to Lidka: 'Say thank you to the gentleman!'

But Lidka had no wish to speak to me.

I never saw her again. Gradually I forgot about her. Meanwhile my practice still grew. The day came when I had a hundred and ten patients. We began at nine in the morning and finished at eight in the evening. Reeling with fatigue, I was taking off my overall when the senior midwife said to me:

'It's the tracheotomy that has brought you all these patients. Do you know what they're saying in the villages? The story goes that when Lidka was ill a steel throat was put into her instead of her own and then sewn up. People go to her village especially to look at her. There's fame for you, doctor. Congratulations.'

'So they think she's living with a steel one now, do they?' I enquired.

'That's right. But you were wonderful, doctor. You did it so coolly, it was marvellous to watch.'

'Hm, well, I never allow myself to worry, you know,' I said, not knowing why. I was too tired even to feel ashamed, so I just looked away. I said goodnight and went home. Snow was falling in large flakes, covering everything, the lantern was lit and my house looked silent, solitary and imposing. As I walked I had only one desire – sleep.

Black as Egypt's Night

Where has the world disappeared to today, my birthday? Where, oh where are the electric lights of Moscow? Where are the people, where is the sky? I look out of my windows at nothing but darkness . . .

We are cut off; the nearest kerosene lanterns are seven miles away at the railway station, and even their flickering light has probably been blown out by the snowstorm. The midnight express to Moscow rushes moaning past and does not even stop; it has no need of this forlorn little halt, buried in snow – except perhaps when the line is blocked by drifts.

The nearest street lamps are thirty-two miles away in the district town. Life there is sweet: it has a cinema, shops. While the snow is whirling and howling out here in the open country, there on the screen, no doubt, the cane-brake is bending to the breeze and palm trees sway as a tropical island comes into view . . .

Meanwhile we are alone.

'Black as Egypt's night,' observed Demyan Lukich, as he raised the blind.

His remarks are somewhat solemn but apt. Egyptian is the word for it.

'Have another glass,' I invited him. (Don't be too hard on us; after all, we – a doctor, a *feldsher* and two midwives – are human too. For months on end we see no one apart from hundreds of sick peasants. We work away, entombed in snow. Surely we may be allowed to drink a couple of glasses of suitably diluted spirit and relish a few of the local sprats on the doctor's birthday?)

'Your health, doctor!' said Demyan Lukich with heartfelt sincerity.

'Here's hoping you survive your stay with us!' said Anna Nikolaevna as she clinked her glass and smoothed her flowered party dress.

Raising her glass, Pelagea Ivanovna took a sip and then squatted down on her haunches to poke the stove. The hot gleam lit up our faces and the vodka generated a warm inner glow.

'I simply cannot imagine,' I said indignantly as I watched the shower of sparks raised by the poker, 'what that woman did with so much belladonna. The whole story sounds insane!'

Feldsher and midwives smiled as they remembered what had happened. At morning surgery that day a red-faced peasant woman of about thirty had elbowed her way into my consulting room. She had bowed to the gynaecological chair which stood behind me, then produced from the front of her dress a wide-necked medicine bottle and crooned ingratiatingly:

'Thanks very much for the medicine, doctor. It did me so much good. Please may I have another bottle?'

I took the bottle from her, and as I glanced at the label a green film passed across my vision. On the label was written in Demyan Lukich's sprawling hand: 'Tinct. Belladonnae . . . etc. 16th December 1916'.

In other words, yesterday I had prescribed for this woman a hefty measure of belladonna and today, my birthday, 17 December, the woman had come back with an empty bottle and a request for more.

'You . . . you . . . you mean to say you drank all this yesterday?' I asked, appalled.

'All of it, sir, all of it,' said the woman in her comfortable, sing-song voice. 'And God bless you for it . . . half the bottle when I got home and the other half when I went to bed. The pain just vanished . . .'

I steadied myself against the gynaecological chair.

'What dose did I tell you?' I croaked. 'I told you five drops at a time . . . What have you done, woman? You've . . . you've . . .'

'I took it, I swear I did!' the woman insisted, thinking I did not believe she had taken my belladonna.

I seized both her ruddy cheeks and stared at her pupils. There as nothing wrong with them. They were rather beautiful and completely normal. Her pulse, too, was excellent. The woman exhibited no signs whatsoever of belladonna poisoning.

'It's impossible!' I said, then shouted: 'Demyan Lukich!'

Demyan Lukich in his white overall appeared from the passage leading to the dispensary.

'Just look what this beauty has done, Demyan Lukich! I don't understand it.'

The peasant woman looked round anxiously, realising that she had done something wrong. Demyan Lukich took the bottle, sniffed it, turned it round in his hands and said sternly:

'You, my dear, are lying. You didn't take this medicine!'

'I swear . . .' she began.

'Don't try and fool us, woman,' Demyan Lukich scolded, pursing his lips. 'We can see through all your little tricks. Own up now – who did you give this medicine to?'

The woman raised her thoroughly normal pupils towards the immaculately whitewashed ceiling and crossed herself.

'May I be . . .'

'Stop it,' growled Demyan Lukich and turned to me: 'This is what they do, doctor. A clever actress like this one here goes to the clinic, we prescribe her some medicine and she goes back home and shares it out among all the women in the village.'

'Oh, sir, how could you . . .'

'Shut up!' the *feldsher* cut her off. 'I've been here eight years and I know. Of course she's been going round every farm and emptying the bottle a few drops at a time,' he went on.

'Give me some more of those drops,' the woman begged in a wheedling tone.

'No, we won't,' I replied as I wiped the sweat from my brow. 'I'm not letting you have any more of *this* medicine. Is your stomach-ache better?'

'Like I said – just vanished!'

'Well, that's good, anyway. I shall give you something else, which will also do you good.' I prescribed the woman some valerian and she left, much disappointed.

This was the incident we discussed sitting in the doctor's quarters on my birthday, while outside the windows were draped with the black curtain of the snowstorm.

'Ah, yes,' said Demyan Lukich, elegantly munching a sardine, 'ah, yes: we're used to that sort of thing here. And you, dear doctor, after all the time you've spent at university and in

Moscow, are going to have to get used to a lot of things. We're living at the back of beyond.'

'Yes, the back of beyond,' came the response like an echo from Anna Nikolaevna.

The snowstorm roared in the chimneys and brushed past the walls. The dark cast-iron of the stove gave off a purple glow. A blessing on the fire which warms medical folk stranded in the depths of the countryside!

'Have you heard about your predecessor Leopold Leopoldovich?' enquired the *feldsher*, as he lit a cigarette, having first politely offered one to Anna Nikolaevna.

'He was a marvellous doctor!' said Pelagea Ivanovna enthusiastically, her eyes gleaming as she stared into the life-giving fire. The imitation brilliants of her Sunday-best comb glinted in her black hair.

'Yes, he was a remarkable personality,' the *feldsher* agreed. 'The peasants literally worshipped him. He had the right approach to them. They were always ready to lie down and be operated on by Liponty. They called him "Liponty Lipontyevich" instead of Leopold Leopoldovich. They had faith in him. And he knew how to talk to them. For instance, his friend Fyodor Kosoi from Dultsevo might come to his surgery. It's like this Liponty Lipontych, he would say, my chest's blocked up so it's hard to draw breath. And besides that, there's a sort of rasping in my throat . . .'

'Laryngitis,' I muttered automatically, having fallen into the habit of lightning diagnosis.

'Quite right. "Well," Liponty would say, "I'll give you something for it which will put you right in a couple of days. There are some French mustard-plasters. Put one on your back between your shoulder-blades, the other on your chest. Keep them on for ten minutes, then take them off. Off you go and do as you're told!"'

'So the man took his mustard-plasters and went. Two days later he was back at the surgery again.

'"Well, what's the matter now?" Liponty asked.

'Kosoi said: "Well, you see, Liponty Lipontyevich, those mustard-plasters didn't do any good."

'"Nonsense!" Liponty replied. "A French mustard-plaster *must* have done you some good. I suppose you never put it on, is that it?"

'"What do you mean – never put it on? It's on still . . ."'
'With that he turned round and there was the mustard-plaster sticking to the back of his sheepskin jerkin!'

I burst into laughter, while Pelagea Ivanovna giggled and poked furiously at a log.

'If you'll forgive me,' I said, 'I think you made that one up! It couldn't have really happened!'

'Made it up? Made it up?' the midwives shouted in chorus.

'I most certainly did not!' the *feldsher* exclaimed bitterly. 'Our life, in fact, is one long string of incidents like that . . . Why, things happen here which . . .'

'What about the sugar?' Anna Nikolaevna exclaimed. 'Tell him about the sugar, Pelagea Ivanovna!'

Closing the stove door and lowering her eyes, Pelagea Ivanovna began:

'One day I went to a confinement at Dultsevo . . .'

'That place Dultsevo is notorious!' the *feldsher* burst out, then apologised: 'Sorry! Do go on, my dear.'

'Well, naturally I examined her,' Pelagea Ivanovna went on, 'and in the birth canal I felt something extraordinary . . . There were some kind of grains or small lumps . . . It turned out to be granulated sugar!'

'How's that for a story!' said Demyan Lukich triumphantly.

'Excuse me, but . . . I don't understand . . .'

'That's peasant women for you!' answered Pelagea Ivanovna. 'She'd been taught by the local wise-woman. She was having a difficult birth, she said, which meant that the baby didn't want to come out into the light of day. She would have to entice it out, so the way to do it was to lure it out with something sweet!'

'Horrors!' I exclaimed.

'When a woman's in labour they give her hair to chew,' said Anna Nikolaevna.

'What on earth for?'

'God alone knows. I've had three confinements where the wretched woman was lying there and spitting something out. Her mouth was full of hair or bristles. Apparently they believe it makes for an easier birth . . .'

The midwives' eyes sparkled as they recounted their experiences. We sat for long by the fire drinking tea, and I listened entranced. Pelagea Ivanovna described how whenever she had to bring an expectant mother from her village to the hospital, she always let her own sleigh travel behind the peasants' sleigh, to prevent them from changing their minds on the way and taking the woman back to her mother; how one day, when a woman had a breech presentation, they had hung her upside down from the ceiling to make the baby turn round; how a woman from Koro-bovo, hearing that it was the practice for doctors to rupture the birth-sac, had cut her baby's head with a table knife so badly that even a man so renowned for his skill as Liponty was unable to save the child and only just managed to save the mother; how . . .

The stove door was long since closed; my guests had departed to their quarters. I noticed that the light shone dully for a while in Anna Nikolaevna's window, then went out. Everything vanished. To the snowstorm was added the impenetrable dark of a December evening, and a black veil shut me off from earth and sky.

I paced up and down my study and the floor creaked under my feet; the room was warmed by a Dutch stove and I could hear a mouse gnawing busily away.

'No,' I reflected, 'I will fight against this Egyptian darkness for as long as fate keeps me here in the wilderness. Granulated sugar . . . ye gods!'

In my reverie by the light of the green-shaded lamp there arose before my mind's eye a great university city, in it a teaching hospital, in the hospital a vast chamber with tiled floor, gleaming taps, sterile white sheets, and a lecturer with a sharp-pointed, greying, very wise-looking beard . . .

A knock heard at such a moment can be alarming, terrifying. I started.

'Who's there, Aksinya?' I asked, leaning over the banisters of the staircase (the doctor's quarters were on two floors: upstairs my study and bedroom, downstairs the dining-room, another room of unknown function and the kitchen, the abode of Aksinya and her husband, the invaluable hospital watchman).

The heavy bolt rumbled, a lighted lamp appeared and bobbed down below, a cold draught blew. Then Aksinya announced:

'It's a patient, a man.'

I was, to tell the truth, delighted. I was not yet ready for sleep and was feeling a little lonely and depressed from the gnawing of the mouse and my own memories. And since it was a man it could not be the worst of all – childbirth.

'Is he walking?'

'Yes,' Aksinya answered, yawning.

'All right, send him into my study.'

The staircase creaked for a long time. The person coming up was a large, heavily-built man. Meanwhile I sat down at my desk trying hard to ensure that my eager twenty-four years did not peep too obviously from behind my professional Aesculapian *persona*. My right hand lay ready on a stethoscope, as though on a revolver.

Through the door sidled a figure, cap in hand, wearing a sheepskin coat and felt boots.

'Why have you come so late in the day?' I asked weightily, to appease my conscience.

'Sorry, doctor,' replied the figure in a gentle, pleasant bass voice. 'The snowstorm's a terror. Held me up, I'm afraid. Couldn't help it, begging your pardon, sir.'

'A polite man,' I thought to myself with pleasure. I liked the figure very much, and even his thick red beard made a favourable impression on me. His beard was clearly the object of considerable care and attention. Its possessor not only combed it but even anointed it with a substance which a doctor, even after such a short spell in the country, could identify without difficulty as clarified butter.

'What's the trouble? Take off your coat. Where are you from?'

The sheepskin coat fell in a mountainous heap on to a chair.

'I've been suffering from a terrible fever,' the patient replied with a doleful look.

'Fever? Aha! Are you from Dultsevo?'

'Yes, sir. I'm the miller.'

'Tell me how it troubles you.'

'Every day at twelve o'clock my head starts to ache, then I seem to get hot all over . . . It makes me shiver for a couple of hours or so and then it goes.'

'Diagnosed already!' rang out triumphantly in my head.

'And the rest of the time you don't feel anything?'

'My legs are a bit weak.'

'Aha. Undo your shirt, please. Hm . . . yes . . .'

When I had finished examining the patient I was delighted by him. After all the incoherent women and frightened adolescents who twitched with horror at the touch of a metal spatula, after that morning's affair of the belladonna, the miller was a sight for my sore, university-trained eyes.

The miller talked sense. What was more, he turned out to be literate, and his every gesture was indicative of respect for the science to which I was devoted – medicine.

'Well, my dear fellow,' I said as I tapped his broad, warm chest, 'you have malaria. Recurrent fever . . . Right now we have a whole ward empty. I strongly advise you to come in for treatment. We can keep you under the necessary observation. I'll start by treating you with powders, and then if that does no good, we'll give you a few injections. Soon put you right. How about it, then?'

'Thank you very much, sir!' the miller replied most politely. 'Heard a lot about you. They're all very satisfied. They say you do them all so much good. I'll gladly have the injections – anything to be cured.'

'Ah, this man is a true ray of light in the darkness!' I thought as I sat down at the desk to write. So doing, my feeling was of such pleasure that it might not have been just any miller but my own brother come for a stay in my hospital.

On one prescription form I wrote:

'Chinini mur. 0.5
D.T. dos. N10
S: Miller Khudov
1 dose in powder form at midnight.'

And signed it with a flourish. On another form I wrote:

'Pelagea Ivanovna, please admit the miller and put him in Ward 2. He has malaria. Quinine in powder form as prescribed to be administered approx. 4 hours before the attack, i.e. at midnight. Here is an exception for you – a literate, intelligent miller!'

When I was already in bed I received a note in reply from the hand of the grumpy, yawning Aksinya:

'Dear doctor, All done. Pel. Ivanovna L.'

I went to sleep . . . and woke up.

'What is it? What? What is it, Aksinya?' I mumbled. Aksinya was standing there, modestly covering herself with her dark-coloured skirt with white polka dots. A flickering wax candle lit up her sleepy, worried features.

'Marya has just come running over – Pelagea Ivanovna has given orders for you to be called at once.'

'What's the matter?'

'She says the miller in Ward 2 is dying.'

'Wha-at? Dying? How can he be *dying*?' For an instant, until I found my slippers, my bare feet felt the chill of the floor. I broke several matches and spent a long time poking them at the wick until it lit with a blue flame. The clock showed exactly six o'clock.

'What's happened? Surely it is malaria and not something else? What on earth can be the matter with him? His pulse was excellent . . .'

No more than five minutes later, with my socks inside out, unkempt, my jacket unbuttoned and wearing felt boots, I bounded across the courtyard, still pitch-dark, and ran to Ward 2.

There on an unmade bed, beside a crumpled heap of bed-clothes, in the light of a small kerosene lamp sat the miller, wearing a hospital nightshirt. His red beard was dishevelled, and his eyes looked to me black and huge. He was swaying like a drunkard, staring about him in terror, breathing heavily . . .

Marya, the nurse, gaped at his purpling face.

Pelagea Ivanovna, her hair down and with her overall only half on, flew towards me.

'Doctor!' she exclaimed in a hoarse voice. 'I swear to you it wasn't my fault! How was anyone to know? You made a point of telling me the man was intelligent.'

'What's happened?'

Pelagea Ivanovna wrung her hands as she said:

'Just imagine, doctor – he swallowed all ten doses of quinine at once! At midnight.'

A murky winter dawn. Demyan Lukich removed the stomach-pump. There was a smell of camphor; on the floor stood a bowl full of reddish-brown liquid. Pale and exhausted, the miller lay wrapped in a white sheet up to his chin, his red beard jutting upwards. I bent over him and felt his pulse to make sure that he would survive the emergency.

'Well, how do you feel?' I enquired.

'Can't see a thing . . . oh . . . ooh . . .' groaned the miller in a faint bass.

'Nor can I,' I answered in some irritation.

'Wassat?' the miller asked (his hearing was still poor).

'Just tell me one thing, old man: why the hell did you do it?' I shouted into his ear.

Glumly and reluctantly came the mumbling answer:

'Well, it seemed a waste of time taking all them powders one at a time. So I thought I'd swallow 'em all at once and be done with it.'

'Incredible!' I exclaimed.

'He must have made it up!' said the *feldsher* in a malicious aside.

'No, I will fight it . . . I will . . . I . . .' After a hard night, sweet sleep overtook me. Darkness, black as Egypt's night, descended and in it I was standing alone, armed with something that might have been a sword or might have been a stethoscope. I was moving forward and fighting . . . somewhere at the back of beyond. But I was not alone. With me was my warrior band: Demyan Lukich, Anna Nikolaevna, Pelagea Ivanovna, all dressed in white overalls, all pressing forward.

Sleep . . . what a boon . . .

Baptism by Rotation

As time passed in my country hospital, I gradually got used to the new way of life.

They were braking flax in the villages as they had always done, the roads were still impassable, and no more than five patients came to my daily surgery. My evenings were entirely free, and I spent them sorting out the library, reading surgical manuals and spending long hours drinking tea alone with the gently humming samovar.

For whole days and nights it poured with rain, the drops pounded unceasingly on the roof and the water cascaded past my window, swirling along the gutter and into a tub. Outside was slush, darkness and fog, through which the windows of the *feldsher's* house and the kerosene lantern over the gateway were no more than faint, blurred patches of light.

On one such evening I was sitting in my study with an atlas of topographical anatomy. The absolute silence was only disturbed by the occasional gnawing of mice behind the sideboard in the dining-room.

I read until my eyelids grew so heavy that they began to stick together. Finally I yawned, put the atlas aside and decided to go to bed. I stretched in pleasant anticipation of sleeping soundly to the accompaniment of the noisy pounding of the rain, then went across to my bedroom, undressed and lay down.

No sooner had my head touched the pillow than there swam hazily before me the face of Anna Prokhorova, a girl of seventeen from the village of Toropovo. She had needed a tooth extracting. Demyan Lukich, the *feldsher*, floated silently past holding a gleaming pair of pincers. Remembering how he always said 'suchlike' instead of 'such' because he was fond of a high-falutin' style, I smiled and fell asleep.

About half an hour later, however, I suddenly woke up as though I had been pinched, sat up, stared fearfully into the darkness and listened.

Someone was drumming loudly and insistently on the outer door and I immediately sensed that those knocks boded no good.

Then came a knock on the door of my quarters.

The noise stopped, there was a grating of bolts, the sound of the cook talking, an indistinct voice in reply, then someone came creaking up the stairs, passed quietly through the study and knocked on my bedroom door.

'Who is it?'

'It's me,' came the reply in a respectful whisper. 'Me, Aksinya, the nurse.'

'What's the matter?'

'Anna Nikolaevna has sent for you. They want you to come to the hospital as quickly as possible.'

'What's happened?' I asked, feeling my heart literally miss a beat.

'A woman has been brought in from Dultsevo. She's having a difficult labour.'

'Here we go!' I thought to myself, quite unable to get my feet into my slippers. 'Hell, the matches won't light. Ah well, it had to happen sooner or later. You can't expect to get nothing but cases of laryngitis or abdominal catarrh all your life.'

'All right, go and tell them I'm coming at once!' I shouted as I got out of bed. Aksinya's footsteps shuffled away from the door and the bolt grated again. Sleep vanished in a moment. Hurriedly, with shaking fingers, I lit the lamp and began dressing. Half past eleven . . . What could be wrong with this woman who was having a difficult birth? Malpresentation? Narrow pelvis? Or perhaps something worse. I might even have to use forceps. Should I send her straight into town? Out of the question! A fine doctor he is, they'll all say. In any case, I have no right to do that. No, I really must do it myself. But do what? God alone knows. It would be disastrous if I lost my head – I might disgrace myself in front of the midwives. Anyway, I must have a look first; no point in getting worried prematurely . . .

I dressed, threw an overcoat over my shoulders, and hoping

that all would be well, ran to the hospital through the rain across
the creaking duckboards. At the entrance I could see a cart in the
semi-darkness, the horse pawing at the rotten boards under its
hooves.

'Did you bring the woman in labour?' I asked the figure
lurking by the horse.

'Yes, that's right . . . we did, sir,' a woman's voice replied
dolefully.

Despite the hour, the hospital was alive and bustling. A
flickering pressure-lamp was burning in the surgery. In the little
passage leading to the delivery room Aksinya slipped past me
carrying a basin. A faint moan came through the door and died
away again. I opened the door and went into the delivery room.
The small, whitewashed room was brightly lit by a lamp in the
ceiling. On a bed alongside the operating table, covered with a
blanket up to her chin, lay a young woman. Her face was
contorted in a grimace of pain and wet strands of hair were
sticking to her forehead. Holding a large thermometer, Anna
Nikolaevna was preparing a solution in a graduated jug, while
Pelagea Ivanovna was getting clean sheets out of the cupboard.
The *feldsher* was leaning against the wall in a Napoleonic pose.
Seeing me, they all jerked into life. The pregnant woman opened
her eyes, wrung her hands and renewed her pathetic, long
drawn-out groaning.

'Well now, what seems to be the trouble?' I asked, sounding
confident.

'Transverse lie,' Anna Nikolaevna answered promptly as she
went on pouring water into the solution.

'I see-ee,' I drawled, and added, frowning: 'Well, let's have a
look . . .'

'Aksinya! Wash the doctor's hands!' snapped Anna Nikolaevna. Her expression was solemn and serious.

As the water flowed, rinsing away the lather from my hands,
reddened from scrubbing, I asked Anna Nikolaevna a few trivial
questions, such as when the woman had been brought in, where
she was from . . . Pelagea Ivanovna's hand turned back the
blanket, I sat down on the edge of the bed and began gently
feeling the swollen belly. The woman groaned, stretched, dug her
fingers into her flesh and crumpled the sheet.

'There, there, relax . . . it won't take long,' I said as I carefully
put my hands to the hot, dry, distended skin.

The fact was that once the experienced Anna Nikolaevna had told me what was wrong, this examination was quite pointless. I could examine the woman as much as I liked, but I would not find out any more than Anna Nikolaevna knew already. Her diagnosis was, of course, correct: transverse lie. It was obvious. Well, what next?

Frowning, I continued palpating the belly on all sides and glanced sidelong at the midwives' faces. Both were watching with intense concentration and their looks registered approval of what I was doing. But although my movements were confident and correct, I did my best to conceal my unease as thoroughly as possible.

'Very well,' I said with a sigh, standing up from the bed, as there was nothing more to be seen from an external examination. 'Let's examine her internally.'

Another look of approval from Anna Nikolaevna.

'Aksinya!'

More water flowed.

'Oh, if only I could consult Döderlein now!' I thought miserably as I soaped my hands. Alas, this was quite impossible. In any case, how could Döderlein help me at a moment like this? I washed off the thick lather and painted my fingers with iodine. A clean sheet rustled in Pelagea Ivanovna's hands and, bending down over the expectant mother, I began cautiously and timidly to carry out an internal examination. Into my mind came an involuntary recollection of the operating theatre in the maternity hospital. Gleaming electric lights in frosted-glass globes, a shining tiled floor, taps and instruments a-glitter everywhere. A junior registrar in a snow-white coat is manipulating the woman, surrounded by three intern assistants, probationers, and a crowd of students doing their practicals. Everything bright, well ordered and safe.

And there was I, all on my own, with a woman in agony on my hands and I was responsible for her. I had no idea, however, what I was supposed to do to help her, because I had seen childbirth at close quarters only twice in my life in a hospital, and both occasions were completely normal. The fact that I was conducting an examination was of no value to me or to the woman; I understood absolutely nothing and could feel nothing of what was inside her.

It was time to make some sort of decision.

'Transverse lie . . . since it's a transverse lie I must . . . I must . . .'

'Turn it round by the foot,' muttered Anna Nikolaevna as though thinking aloud, unable to restrain herself.

An older, more experienced doctor would have looked askance at her for butting in, but I am not the kind to take offence.

'Yes,' I concurred gravely, 'a podalic version.'

The pages of Döderlein flickered before my eyes. Internal method . . . Combined method . . . External method . . . Page after page, covered in illustrations. A pelvis; twisted, crushed babies with enormous heads . . . a little dangling arm with a loop on it.

Indeed I had read it not long ago and had underlined it, soaking up every word, mentally picturing the interrelationship of every part of the whole and every method. And as I read it I imagined that the entire text was being imprinted on my brain for ever.

Yet now only one sentence of it floated back into my memory:

'A transverse lie is a wholly unfavourable position.'

Too true. Wholly unfavourable both for the woman and for a doctor who only qualified six months ago.

'Very well, we'll do it,' I said as I stood up.

Anna Nikolaevna's expression came to life.

'Demyan Lukich,' she turned to the *feldsher*, 'get the chloroform ready.'

It was a good thing that she had said so, because I was still not certain whether the operation was supposed to be done under anaesthesia or not! Of course, under anaesthesia – how else?

Still, I must have a look at Döderlein . . .

As I washed my hands I said:

'All right, then . . . prepare her for anaesthesia and make her comfortable. I'll be back in a moment; I must just go to my room and fetch some cigarettes.'

'Very good, doctor, we'll be ready by the time you come back,' replied Anna Nikolaevna.

I dried my hands, the nurse threw my coat over my shoulders and without putting my arms into the sleeves I set off for home at a run.

In my study I lit the lamp and, forgetting to take off my cap, rushed straight to the bookcase.

There it was – Döderlein's *Operative Obstetrics*. I began hastily to leaf through the glossy pages.

'. . . version is always a dangerous operation for the mother . . .'

A cold shiver ran down my spine.

'The chief danger lies in the possibility of a spontaneous rupture of the uterus . . .'

Spon-tan-e-ous . . .

'If in introducing his hand into the uterus the obstetrician encounters any hindrances to penetrating to the foot, whether from lack of space or as a result of a contraction of the uterine wall, he should refrain from further attempts to carry out the version . . .'

Good. Provided I am able, by some miracle, to recognise these 'hindrances' and I refrain from 'further attempts', what, might I ask, am I then supposed to do with an anaesthetised woman from the village of Dultsevo?
Further:

'It is absolutely impermissible to attempt to reach the feet by penetrating behind the back of the foetus . . .'

Noted.

'It must be regarded as erroneous to grasp the upper leg, as doing so may easily result in the foetus being revolved too far; this can cause the foetus to suffer a severe blow, which can have the most deplorable consequences . . .'

'Deplorable consequences.' Rather a vague phrase, but how sinister. What if the husband of the woman from Dultsevo is left a widower? I wiped the sweat from my brow, rallied my strength and disregarded all the terrible things that could go wrong, trying only to remember the absolute essentials: what I had to do, where and how to put my hands. But as I ran my eye over the lines of black print, I kept encountering new horrors. They leaped out at me from the page.

'. . . in view of the extreme danger of rupture . . .'
'. . . the internal and combined methods must be classified as among the most dangerous obstetric operations to which a mother can be subjected . . .'

And as a grand finale:

'. . . with every hour of delay the danger increases . . .'

That was enough. My reading had borne fruit: my head was in a complete muddle. For a moment I was convinced that I understood nothing, and above all that I had no idea what sort of version I was going to perform: combined, bi-polar, internal, external . . .

I abandoned Döderlein and sank into an armchair, struggling to reduce my random thoughts to order. Then I glanced at my watch. Hell! I had already spent twenty minutes in my room, and they were waiting for me.

'. . . with every hour of delay . . .'

Hours are made up of minutes, and at times like this the minutes fly past at insane speed. I threw Döderlein aside and ran back to the hospital.

Everything there was ready. The *feldsher* was standing over a little table preparing the anaesthetic mask and the chloroform bottle. The expectant mother already lay on the operating table. Her ceaseless moans could be heard all over the hospital.

'There now, be brave,' Pelagea Ivanovna muttered consolingly as she bent over the woman, 'the doctor will help you in a moment.'

'Oh, no! I haven't the strength . . . No . . . I can't stand it!'

'Don't be afraid,' whispered the midwife. 'You'll stand it. We'll just give you something to sniff, and then you won't feel anything.'

Water gushed noisily from the taps as Anna Nikolaevna and I began washing and scrubbing our arms bared to the elbow. Against a background of groans and screams Anna Nikolaevna described to me how my predecessor, an experienced surgeon, had performed versions. I listened avidly to her, trying not to miss a single word. Those ten minutes told me more than everything I had read on obstetrics for my qualifying exams, in which I had actually passed the obstetrics paper 'with distinction'. From her brief remarks, unfinished sentences and passing hints I learned the essentials which are not to be found in any textbooks. And by the time I had begun to dry the perfect whiteness and cleanliness of my hands with sterile gauze, I was seized with confidence and a firm and absolutely definite plan had formed in my mind. There was simply no need to bother any longer over whether it was to be a combined or bi-polar version.

None of these learned words meant anything at that moment. Only one thing mattered: I had to put one hand inside, assist the version with the other hand from outside and without relying on books but on common sense, without which no doctor is any good, carefully but firmly bring one foot downwards and pull the baby after it.

I had to be calm and cautious yet at the same time utterly decisive and unfaltering.

'Right, off you go,' I instructed the *feldsher* as I began painting my fingers with iodine.

At once Pelagea Ivanovna folded the woman's arms and the *feldsher* clamped the mask over her agonised face. Chloroform slowly began to drip out of the dark yellow glass bottle, and the room started to fill with the sweet, nauseous odour. The expressions of the *feldsher* and midwives hardened with concentration, as though inspired . . .

'Haaa! Ah!' The woman suddenly shrieked. For a few seconds she writhed convulsively, trying to force away the mask.

'Hold her!'

Pelagea Ivanovna seized her by the arms and lay across her chest. The woman cried out a few more times, jerking her face away from the mask. Her movements slowed down, although she mumbled dully:

'Oh . . . let me go . . . ah . . .'

She grew weaker and weaker. The white room was silent. The translucent drops continued to drip, drip, drip on to the white gauze.

'Pulse, Pelagea Ivanovna?'

'Firm.'

Pelagea Ivanovna raised the woman's arm and let it drop: as lifeless as a leather thong, it flopped on to the sheet. Removing the mask, the *feldsher* examined the pupil of her eye.

'She's asleep.'

A pool of blood. My arms covered in blood up to the elbows. Bloodstains on the sheets. Red clots and lumps of gauze. Pelagea Ivanovna shaking and slapping the baby, Aksinya rattling buckets as she poured water into basins.

The baby was dipped alternately into cold and hot water. He did not make a sound, his head flopping lifelessly from side to side as though on a thread. Then suddenly there came a noise somewhere between a squeak and a sigh, followed by the first weak, hoarse cry.

'He's alive . . . alive . . .' mumbled Pelagea Ivanovna as she laid the baby on a pillow.

And the mother was alive. Fortunately nothing had gone wrong. I felt her pulse. Yes, it was firm and steady; the *feldsher* gently shook her by the shoulder as he said:

'Wake up now, my dear.'

The bloodstained sheets were thrown aside and the mother hastily covered with a clean one before the *feldsher* and Aksinya wheeled her away to the ward. The swaddled baby was borne away on his pillow, the brown, wrinkled little face staring out from its white wrapping as he cried ceaselessly in a thin, pathetic whimper.

Water gushing from the taps of the sluice. Anna Nikolaevna coughed as she dragged hungrily at a cigarette.

'You did the version well, doctor. You seemed very confident.'

Scrubbing furiously at my hands, I glanced sidelong at her: was she being sarcastic? But no, her expression was a sincere one of pride and satisfaction. My heart was brimming with joy. I glanced round at the white and bloodstained disorder, at the red water in the basin and felt that I had won. But somewhere deep down there wriggled a worm of doubt.

'Let's wait and see what happens now,' I said.

Anna Nikolaevna turned to look at me in astonishment.

'What can happen? Everything's all right.'

I mumbled something vague in reply. What I had meant to say was to wonder whether the mother was really safe and sound, whether I might not have done her some harm during the operation . . . the thought nagged dully at my mind. My knowledge of obstetrics was so vague, so fragmentary and bookish. What about a rupture? How would it show? And when would it show – now or, perhaps, later? Better not talk about that.

'Well, almost anything,' I said. 'The possibility of infection cannot be ruled out,' I added, repeating the first sentence from some textbook that came into my mind.

'Oh, tha-at,' Anna Nikolaevna drawled complacently. 'Well,

with luck nothing of that sort will happen. How could it, anyway? Everything here is clean and sterile.'

It was after one o'clock when I went back to my room. In a pool of light on the desk in my study lay Döderlein open at the page headed 'Dangers of Version'. For another hour after that, sipping my cooling tea, I sat over it, turning the pages. And an interesting thing happened: all the previously obscure passages became entirely comprehensible, as though they had been flooded with light; and there, at night, under the lamplight in the depth of the countryside I realised what real knowledge was.

'One can gain a lot of experience in a country practice,' I thought as I fell asleep, 'but even so one must go on and on reading, reading . . . more and more . . .'

The Speckled Rash

'This is it!' Intuition prompted me. No need to rely on my knowledge; as a doctor only six months qua lified, I had none.

Afraid to touch the man's bare, warm shoulder (though there was nothing to fear), I said to him from where I stood:

'Just move nearer to the light, would you?'

He turned the way I wanted him to, and the light of the kerosene pressure-lamp shone on his yellow-tinged skin. A white, speckled rash showed through the yellow colouring of his flanks and bulging chest. 'Like stars in the sky,' I thought to myself with a chill of fear as I bent down to his chest. Then I drew my eyes away from it and up to his face. Before me was a man of about forty with an untidy, ashen-grey beard and bright little eyes under swollen lids. To my great amazement I saw in those eyes a look of dignity and a sense of his own importance. Bored and indifferent, he blinked occasionally as he adjusted the belt of his trousers.

'This is it – syphilis,' I repeated grimly to myself. This was my first professional encounter with it, as I had been flung straight from university into a remote village.

I stumbled on this case of syphilis by chance. The patient had come to me complaining of a congested throat. All unawares, without a thought of syphilis, I had told him to get undressed, and only then did I see the speckled rash.

Putting all the symptoms together – his hoarseness, the sinister inflammation of his throat, the strange white patches on it and his mottled chest – I guessed at the trouble. My first, cowardly reaction was to rub my hands with a ball of sublimate of mercury.

The minute it took to do this was poisoned by the anxious thought that he might have coughed on my hands. Then weakly and squeamishly I rolled a glass spatula in my hands and inspected my patient's throat with it. Where should I put the spatula? I decided to place it on a wad of cotton wool on the window ledge.

'Well now,' I said, 'you see . . . er . . . it seems . . . in fact it's quite certain . . . you see, you have a rather unpleasant disease – you have syphilis . . .'

As soon as I had said this I felt awkward. I thought he might be frightened out of his wits. But not at all. He gave me a sidelong glance, rather as a hen looks up with her round eye when she hears a voice calling her. I was astonished to see mistrust in his round eye.

'You've got syphilis,' I repeated softly.

'What's that, then?' asked the man with the speckled rash.

I had a brief, sharp mental vision of a snow-white ward at the university hospital, a lecture-theatre filled with rows of students' heads and the grey beard of the professor of venereology . . . But I quickly came to myself and remembered that I was about a thousand miles away from the lecture-theatre and thirty miles from the nearest railway, and that my only light was a kerosene lamp . . . I could hear the dull buzz of voices coming from my numerous patients waiting their turn on the other side of the white door. Outside the window, night was steadily drawing in and the first winter snow was flying on the wind.

I made my patient take off more clothes and found a primary lesion which was already healing. I was no longer in any doubt, and felt the pride which invariably arose inside me whenever I made a correct diagnosis.

'You can get dressed again,' I said. 'You've got syphilis! It is an extremely serious illness which affects the whole body. It will take a long time to cure.'

Here I faltered because – I swear it – I detected in that hen-like gaze astonishment clearly mixed with derision.

'But I'm only a bit hoarse in the throat,' said the patient.

'Yes, I know. That's *why* it's gone hoarse, and that's why you've got a rash on your chest. Have a look at your chest.'

He squinted at his chest. The ironic glint in his eyes did not fade.

'Couldn't you just give me something for my throat?' he asked.

'Why does he keep on like this?' I thought somewhat impatiently. 'I'm talking about syphilis and all he worries about is his throat!'

'Look here,' I continued aloud, 'your throat is a minor matter. We'll make your throat better too, but the most important thing is to get rid of the general disease. And the treatment's going to take a long time – two years.'

At this the patient stared at me. I saw the verdict in his eyes: You've gone off your head, doctor!

'Why so long?' he asked. 'How can it take two years? All I need is something to gargle for my throat.'

I saw red. I started to speak. I was no longer afraid of frightening him. Oh, no; on the contrary, I even hinted that his nose might drop off. I told him what the future held for him if he did not take the necessary treatment. I mentioned how contagious syphilis was and spoke at length about plates, spoons and cups, and about separate towels.

'Are you married?' I said.

'Yes, I am,' he answered in amazement.

'Send your wife to me immediately!' I said heatedly. 'I suppose she's sick too, isn't she?'

'Send the wife?' he asked, looking at me in great astonishment.

We went on in this vein. He kept blinking and looking into my eyes, and I into his. It was, in fact, less of a conversation than a monologue – a brilliant monologue by me, which would have earned a final year student the highest marks from any professor. I discovered that I was a mine of information on syphilis. My unexpected resourcefulness filled in the lacunae of all those passages where the German and Russian textbooks fail to go into detail. I told him what happens to the bones of an untreated syphilitic and sketched en passant an outline of progressive paralysis. Then there were his offspring – and how was his wife to be saved? Or if she was already infected, which she was bound to be, how was she to be treated?

In the end my torrent of words dried up and I self-consciously took out of my pocket a reference book in a red binding with gold lettering. It was my faithful friend, and I was never parted from it in those first stages of my difficult career. How many times did it come to my rescue when the accursed problem of prescriptions gaped before me like a black abyss! While the patient was getting dressed I furtively leafed through its pages and found what I needed.

Mercury ointment is a great remedy!

'You must rub this stuff on you. You'll be given six little bags of ointment. You'll rub on one bagful a day, like this . . .'

I gave a vigorous demonstration of how to do it, rubbing my overall with my open palm.

'Today you must rub it on your arm, tomorrow on your leg, then on the other arm. When you've rubbed it on six times, wash it all off and come and see me. Without fail. Do you hear? Without fail! And apart from this, you must take great care of your teeth and your mouth in general while you are under treatment. I'll give you a mouthwash. After meals you must be certain to rinse out your mouth.'

'And my throat?' he asked hoarsely, and at once I noticed that he only came to life at the word 'mouthwash'.

'Yes, yes, your throat too.'

A few minutes later the yellow back of his sheepskin jerkin was disappearing through the door and a woman in a headscarf was elbowing past him. A few minutes later, as I ran along the half-dark passage from my out-patient surgery to get some cigarettes from the pharmacist, I happened to overhear a hoarse whisper:

'He's no good. Young fellow. I've just got a sore throat, see, but he looks me all over . . . chest, belly . . . I've more than enough work on my hands and it took me half a day to get to the hospital. By the time I get back it'll be dark. Lord, here am I with nothing but a sore throat and he gives me ointment for my legs.'

'Careless, careless,' a quavering peasant woman's voice agreed, and then suddenly stopped short as I flitted past like an apparition in my white overall. I could not help looking round, and in the semi-darkness I recognised the little beard looking as if it were made of tow, the heavy eyelids, the hen-like eyes and the ferociously hoarse voice. I pulled my head into my shoulders and furtively tried to hunch myself up as if I were guilty, and disappeared with a burning sense of resentment. I was in a terrible state.

Had I been completely wasting my time?

I refused to believe it. Every morning for a month I studied the reception book as keenly as a detective, expecting to come across the surname of the wife of the man who had listened so attentively to my monologue on syphilis. I waited for the man himself for a whole month. He never came back. When a month had passed the memory of him faded, I stopped worrying and forgot him. Because there was always something new, and every working day in those remote backwoods brought unexpected and difficult cases which forced me to overtax my brain; countless times I would be reduced to utter perplexity, only to recover my presence of mind and return to the struggle with new zest.

Now that many years have passed and I am far from that remote hospital with its peeling white walls, I cast my mind back to the speckled rash on his chest. Where is he? What is he doing? Don't tell me, I know. If he is still alive, he and his wife are visiting the ramshackle old hospital from time to time. They are complaining of lesions on their legs. I can clearly picture him unwrapping his foot-cloths and looking for sympathy. The young doctor, who may be a man or a woman, in a patched overall, is bending over his legs, pressing his fingers on the bone above the lesion and looking for the cause. He finds it, writes in his book: 'Lues III', and then asks whether he has ever been prescribed black ointment.

And then, just as I remember him now, he will remember me, the year 1917, snow outside the window and six little bags of waxed paper, six sticky unused lumps.

'Yes, he did give me some,' he will say, and this time his expression will no longer be ironical but full of dread. The doctor will write out a prescription for potassium iodide or maybe some other treatment. And maybe he will take a glance at his reference book just as I did . . .

Greetings, dear colleague!

'. . . and then, dearest wife, give my kindest regards to Safron Ivanovich. And apart from that, dear wife, go and see our doctor because for the last six months I have been suffering from a foul and painful disease, syphilis. I didn't tell you when I was with you. Take the treatment for it.

Your husband, Anatoly Bukov.'

The young woman pressed a corner of her flannel shawl to her mouth, sat down on the bench and shook with sobs. Her fair curls, wet with melted snow, lay across her forehead.

'Isn't he a swine?' she cried.

'Yes, he is,' I answered firmly.

Then followed the most difficult and agonising part of her visit. I had to calm her; but how was I to do it? We whispered for a long time to the accompaniment of the rumble of impatient voices in the waiting room. My soul was not yet blunted to human suffering and from somewhere in its depths I was able to find comforting words. First of all I tried to banish her fear. I told her that so far nothing was definite and she must not give way to despair before she had been examined. Even then there was no cause for despair; I told her with what success this terrible disease was nowadays being treated.

'The swine,' the young woman sobbed and choked on her tears.

'Yes, he's a swine,' I echoed.

We spent quite a long time swearing at this 'dearest husband' who had spent a short time at home and then left for Moscow. In the end the woman's tears began to dry, leaving stains on her face and swollen eyelids over her dark despairing eyes.

'What am I going to do? I have two children,' she said in a husky, exhausted voice.

'Wait, wait,' I mumbled. 'We'll see what has to be done.'

I called the midwife, Pelagea Ivanovna, and the three of us retired to a separate ward where there was a gynaecological chair.

'The scoundrel,' Pelagea Ivanovna hissed through her teeth. The woman was silent, her eyes two black pits staring out of the window at the twilight.

It was one of the most thorough examinations I have ever made. Pelagea Ivanovna and I did not miss an inch of her body. But nowhere could I find anything suspicious.

'Do you know,' I said, hoping passionately that this was not wishful thinking and that we should not later find the sinister, hard, primary chancre: 'Do you know what? You can stop worrying! There's hope. Yes, there is. Of course there's still a chance that it might develop, but right now there's nothing wrong with you.'

'Nothing?' the woman asked hoarsely. 'Nothing?' Her eyes began to shine and her cheekbones flushed with colour. 'But say it begins?'

'I can't understand it myself,' I said under my breath to Pelagea Ivanovna. 'According to what she's told us, she ought to be infected. But there's nothing.'

'Nothing at all,' Pelagea Ivanovna repeated after me.

We spent another few minutes whispering about dates and various intimate matters and I told the woman she would have to come regularly to the hospital.

As I looked at her then I saw that she was crushed. Hope had crept in and almost immediately vanished. She burst into tears and went away like a dark shadow. From that time on she lived under a sword of Damocles. Every Saturday she came silently to my surgery. She lost a lot of weight and her cheekbones protruded more sharply, her eyes became sunken and encircled by shadows. She would untie her shawl with a habitual movement and we would all three go to the ward to examine her.

The first three Saturdays passed and we found nothing. Then gradually she started to recover. Her eyes regained their sparkle, her face livened and the drawn look began to smooth out. The odds rose in our favour. The danger was passing. On the fourth Saturday I spoke with certainty. I could count on a roughly ninety per cent chance of a favourable outcome. The first twenty-one-day period was well past. There remained the remote possibility that the chancre might develop extremely late. That period finally passed too, and one day, as I threw the shiny mirror away into the basin, having felt her glands for the last time, I said to the woman:

'You are no longer in any danger. You needn't come any more. You have been lucky.'

'I'm all right?' she asked in an unforgettable voice.

'Yes, you're fine.'

I lack the power to describe her face. I remember that she bowed low from the waist and went out.

She did, however, come once more. She was holding a bundle in her arms – two pounds of butter and two dozen eggs. After a terrible inner struggle, I accepted neither. Being so young, I felt very proud of this. But later, when I had to go without food in the years immediately after the revolution, I often thought of the kerosene lamp, those dark eyes, and the golden slab of butter marked with fingerprints and with droplets of water oozing out of it like dew.

But why should I recall this woman, condemned to four months of terror, when so many years have passed since then? There is a reason. For she was my second suspected syphilis patient and I later devoted the best years of my life to venereal diseases. The first was the man with the speckled rash on his chest. She was the second, and the only exception, because she was afraid: the only one to remain in my memory from all the work that we four (Pelagea Ivanovna, Anna Nikolaevna, Demyan Lukich and myself) did by the light of those kerosene lamps.

While she was going through her agonizing Saturday visits as if waiting for her execution, I started investigating the disease. The long autumn evenings and the hot tiled stove produced such warmth and stillness that I felt all alone in the world with my lamp. Somewhere outside life was raging like a storm, but here only the slanting rain could be heard tapping at my window, then turning imperceptibly into soundless snow. I sat for long hours studying the last five years' records of the out-patients' surgery. The names of people and villages passed before me in their thousands and tens of thousands. I was looking for syphilis in these columns of people and I came across it often. There were rows of boring, routine entries like 'Bronchitis', 'Laryngitis', and others . . . But here it was: 'Lues III'. And in the margin in the same bold hand:

'R. Ung. hydrarg. ciner. 3.0 D.t.d.'

That was it – the black ointment.

And off I would go again. Again the bronchitis and catarrh would dance before my eyes and then suddenly there would be a break . . . 'Lues' again.

The more frequent entries, in fact, were of secondary syphilis. Tertiary cases occurred less often, and then potassium iodide was boldly written in the 'Treatment' column.

The more I read the old mildew-smelling folios of the out-patients' register which I had retrieved from the attic, the more light filtered into my inexperienced head. I began to understand some appalling things.

Where, for instance, were the entries for primary lesions? Somehow there did not seem to be any. There was hardly a single one among a thousand names. What could this mean?

'This means,' I said in the dark to myself and to the mouse that was nibbling the backs of the old books on the shelves, 'this means that the people here have no conception of syphilis and the lesions don't frighten them. I see. And then they heal spontaneously, leaving a scar. And is that all? No, that's not all! For then secondary syphilis, the vicious stage, sets in. Semyon Khotov, aged 32, will get a sore throat and oozing papules and then he will go to the hospital and he will be given the grey ointment . . .'

The light cast by my lamp formed a circle on the table and the chocolate-coloured woman lying on the bottom of the ashtray had vanished under the pile of cigarette butts.

'I'll find this Semyon Khotov. Let's see now . . .' The slightly yellowing pages of the out-patients' register crackled faintly. On 17 June 1916 Semyon Khotov was given six bags of mercury ointment, invented long ago to heal people like him. I can imagine my predecessor saying to Semyon as he handed him the ointment:

'Semyon, when you've rubbed it on six times, wash it all off and come and see me again. Do you hear me, Semyon?'

Semyon bowed, of course, and thanked the doctor in a hoarse voice. Well, in another ten to twelve days he is bound to appear in the book again. Let's see . . . Cigarette smoke, rustle of pages. Hmm . . . not a sign of him! He's not there ten days later, nor twenty. He's not there at all. Poor Semyon Khotov. In all likelihood the speckled rash has vanished like the stars at dawn and the condylomata have dried up. And Semyon will surely perish. I shall probably see him at my surgery with gummatous lesions. Is the bridge of his nose still intact? Are the pupils of his eyes symmetrical? Poor Semyon!

But whom have we here? Not Semyon Khotov, but Ivan Karpov. Nothing surprising in that. Why shouldn't Karpov fall ill? Yes, but wait a minute – why has he been prescribed calomel with sugar and milk in small doses? The reason is that Ivan is two years old! And he is suffering from 'Lues II'. That fateful 'II'! He was covered in a rash when his mother carried him in and he struggled out of the doctor's strong grasp. It is all quite clear.

'I know, I can guess. Now I realise where the two-year-old had the primary lesion which always precedes the secondary stage. It was in the mouth! He got it from his spoon.'

What lessons there are to be learned from the backwoods, from the peace and quiet of country life! Yes, the old register has many interesting things to tell the young doctor.

Above Ivan Karpov there was written:

'Avdotya Karpova, aged 39.'

Who was she? Oh, I see. She was Ivan's mother. She was carrying him as he cried.

And below Ivan Karpov:

'Maria Karpova, aged 8.'

Who's that? His sister. More calomel . . .

The whole family is there. A family. There's only one member missing – Karpov, 35 to 40 years old. His first name is not known. Was it Sidor, Pyotr . . . ? Anyway, it doesn't matter.

Ah, here's the document. Now I see. He probably came back from the damned war and did not 'confess', or maybe he did not know that he needed to. Then he went away again. And that's how it began. After Avdotya, Maria; after Maria, Ivan. They used the same soup bowls and towels.

Here's another family. And another. There's an old man, seventy years old. 'Lues II'. An old man. What had he done wrong? Nothing. He had simply shared a mug; non-sexual contagion. It was daylight outside, with the whitish light of an early December dawn. I had sat up the whole lonely night poring over the hospital records and the splendid German textbooks with their colourful illustrations.

On my way to the bedroom I mumbled through a yawn:

'I'm going to fight this thing.'

In order to fight it I had to see it. And it was not long in coming. A sleigh road had been laid, and on some days as many as a hundred patients came to see me. The day would begin in cloudy white light and end with a black haze into which the last sleighs would disappear with a mysterious hiss.

It came in many insidious guises. It would take the form of whitish lesions in an adolescent girl's throat, or of bandy legs, or of deep-seated, indolent ulcers on an old woman's yellow legs, or of oozing papules on the body of a woman in her prime. Sometimes it proudly displayed itself on the forehead as a crescent-shaped 'crown of Venus', or, as an indirect punishment for the sins of their fathers, on children with noses that were the shape of a Cossack's saddle. And there were other times when it simply escaped my attention. I was only just out of the lecture-theatre, after all!

Unaided and alone I thought it all out for myself. Somewhere the disease was lurking in people's bones and in their minds. I learned a great deal.

'They told me to rub some stuff on.'

'Was it black ointment?'

'That's it, sir, black ointment.'
'On alternate limbs? On the arm one day, on the leg the next?'
'So he did. How did you know?' (flatteringly).
How could I fail to know? It was all so obvious. Just look at that gumma!
'Were you in great pain?'
'I should think so! Howled more than a woman having a baby.'
'Uhuh . . . did you have a sore throat?'
'That's right. I had a sore throat. Last year.'
'I see. Did Leopold Leopoldovich give you the ointment?'
'That's right. Black as my boot, it was.'
'Well, you made a bad job of rubbing it on. You didn't do it properly . . .'
I wasted countless kilograms of grey ointment. I prescribed masses of potassium iodide and used a great deal of strong language. I managed to persuade a few to come back after they had rubbed on the first six bagfuls of ointment. A few of these actually underwent the initial course of injections, although most did not complete them. The majority slipped through my fingers like sand in an hourglass, and I could not go looking for them out in the snowbound darkness. I became convinced that syphilis was so fearful here precisely because it was not feared. And that is why, at the beginning of these reminiscences, I introduced the woman with the dark eyes. I remember her with a kind of heartfelt respect for her very fear. But she was the only one!
As I matured, I grew more single-minded and sometimes even sullen. I dreamed of when my spell in that job would be over and I could return to the university town, where it would be easier to fight syphilis.
On one such gloomy day a very good-looking young woman came to my surgery at the hospital holding a swaddled baby in her arms. Two toddlers stumbled in after her, hindered by their oversized felt boots as they hung on to the blue skirt which flared out from under her sheepskin jacket.
'The children have suddenly come out in a rash,' the pink-cheeked woman said gravely.
Cautiously I touched the forehead of the little girl who was holding on to the skirt. She hid herself in its folds and vanished without trace. I fished out the fat-faced little boy from behind the other side of the skirt and felt him too. Both their foreheads felt quite normal.

'Would you undress the baby, my dear?'

She unwrapped the baby girl. Her naked little body was spattered with a starry rash like the sky on a frosty night. It was covered from head to foot in roseola and oozing papules. Vanka, the little boy, suddenly struggled out of my grip and started to howl. Demyan Lukich came to help me.

'It's a chill, isn't it?' said the mother, looking at me with a serene expression.

'A chill!' Lukich growled and made a grimace of pity and disgust. 'The whole damn district of Korobovo has caught this sort of chill.'

'What's it from?' the mother asked while I inspected her mottled sides and chest.

'Get dressed,' I said.

Then I sat down at the desk, laid my head on my hand and yawned (she was one of the last that day; she was number ninety-eight). Then I said:

'Both you, my dear, and your children are very, very ill. This is a dreadful, dangerous disease. You must start a very long course of treatment at once.'

What a pity that words are so inadequate to describe the incredulity in the woman's bulging eyes. She turned the baby over like a log in her arms, stared dully at its legs and asked:

'Where does it come from?'

And she gave a crooked grin.

'That's not the point,' I replied, lighting my fiftieth cigarette that day. 'You should be asking what will happen to your children if you don't have them treated.'

'Nothin' at all, that's what,' she answered and started wrapping the baby in its swaddling clothes.

My watch lay on the table in front of me. As far as I remember, by the time I had been speaking for three minutes the woman burst into sobs. I was very glad of these tears, brought on by my intentionally cruel and frightening words, because it was only thanks to them that I was able to say what I said next:

'So they're staying. Demyan Lukich, put them in the annexe, please. I shall go to town tomorrow and get permission to open an in-patient section for syphilitics.'

The *feldsher* showed a lively interest:

'But doctor – (he was a great sceptic) – how shall we manage on our own? What about the medicines? We can't spare any nurses . . . and who's going to do the cooking? Have you thought about the crockery, the syringes?'

But I shook my head obstinately and answered:

'I'll see to all that.'

A month passed.

The three rooms of the snow-covered annexe were lit by lamps with tin shades. The beds were made up with torn old sheets. There were only two syringes – a small one-gramme syringe and a five-gramme venereal one. In other words, it was pitiful, snowbound poverty. But one syringe was proudly kept separate – the instrument with which, inwardly dying of fear, I had already administered several difficult and unfamiliar injections of the new Salvarsan.

More than that: I was feeling much relieved, as seven men and five women were lying in the annexe, and each day their speckled rashes were melting before my eyes.

It was evening. Demyan Lukich was holding a small lamp and casting its light on the shy little boy, Vanka, whose mouth was smeared with semolina. But the boy no longer had a rash. It was balm to my conscience as all four of them passed under the lamp.

'I think I'll get myself discharged tomorrow,' said the mother, tucking in her blouse.

'No, you mustn't go yet,' I replied. 'You must still have another course of injections.'

'I won't agree to it,' she retorted. 'I've got too much to do at home. Thank you for your help, but please discharge me tomorrow. We're better now.'

Our conversation gradually became so heated that we both lost our tempers. It ended like this:

'Do you know what you are?' I said, feeling my face redden. 'You're a . . . fool!'

'What sort of language is that? Do you always swear at your patients?'

'You're much worse than a fool! You're not that, you're a . . . ! Take a look at your Vanka! Are you trying to kill him? Well, I'm not going to let you!'

She stayed another ten days.

Ten days! Wild horses could not have kept her longer. But believe me, my conscience was clear and I was not even worried about calling her a fool. I'm not sorry. What is swearing in comparison with the speckled rash!

Many years have passed since then. Fate and the turbulent years have put a long distance between me and the snow-covered annexe. What is happening there and who is there now? I am certain it has been improved. The building has probably been whitewashed and there are new sheets. There is no electricity, of course. It is just possible that as I write these lines a young head is bending over a patient's chest. The yellow light from a kerosene lamp is shining on a yellow leg.

Greetings, dear colleague!

The Blizzard

Now howls the blizzard like a wolf,
Now, child-like, whimpers, sobs and weeps.

According to the omniscient Aksinya, the whole story began when a clerk called Palchikov, who lived in Shalometyevo, fell in love with the daughter of an agronomist. His was a flaming passion, which consumed the poor wretch's heart. He drove into the nearby town of Grachyovka and ordered himself a suit. The effect was dazzling, and it may well be that the grey stripes of that clerk's new trousers sealed the luckless man's fate. The agronomist's daughter agreed to become his wife.

I had acquired such fame after amputating the leg of the girl who fell into a flax-brake that I almost expired under the burden of my reputation. Every day a hundred peasants would drive up the sleigh track to attend my surgery. I stopped having lunch. Arithmetic is a cruel science: assuming that I spent no more than five minutes on each patient . . . five! . . . then five hundred minutes equals eight hours and twenty minutes – without a break, please note. Apart from that I had a ward for forty in-patients. And I also did operations.

In short, when I left the hospital at nine o'clock in the evening I had no desire to eat, drink or sleep. My only wish was for no one to call me out to a confinement. And in two weeks I was dragged out at night along that sleigh track five times.

A film of liquid clouded my eyes and a vertical fold, like a worm, appeared above the bridge of my nose. At night through a dim haze I dreamed of failed operations and exposed ribs, of my

hands covered in human blood, and I would wake up in a cold
sweat despite the heat from my tiled stove.

On my rounds I would march urgently round the ward, followed by a male and two female assistants. As I stopped at the
bedside of a sick man, dripping with fever and wheezing miserably, I would force my brain to disgorge everything that was in it.
My fingers would feel the hot, dry skin, I would examine his
pupils, tap his ribs, listen to the deep-down, mysterious beat of
the heart, all the while obsessed by one thought – how can I save
him? And how can I save the next patient – and the next . . . ?
All of them!

It was like a battle, which began every morning by the pale
light reflected from the snow and ended by the fitful yellow gleam
of a pressure-lamp.

'How will all this end, I'd like to know?' I said to myself one
night. 'The sleighs will keep on coming all through January,
February and March.'

I wrote to Grachyovka politely reminding them that my practice was supposed to be manned by a second doctor.

The letter set off on its twenty-five-mile journey by wood-
sledge across an ocean of snow. Three days later came the reply:
they said yes, of course, of course, definitely, only not at present
. . . no one would be coming for the time being . . .

The letter ended with a few flattering comments on my work
and good wishes for my continued success.

Inspired by those remarks I returned to swabbing, injecting
diphtheria serum, lancing abscesses of monstrous proportions,
applying plastercasts.

On Tuesday there were not a hundred but a hundred and eleven
out-patients. I finished my surgery at nine o'clock in the evening
and fell asleep trying to guess how many there would be on Wed-
nesday. I dreamed that nine hundred people came.

There was something unusually white about the morning light
as it shone through my window. I opened my eyes, unaware of
what had woken me up. Then I realised what it was: someone
was knocking.

'Doctor . . .' I recognised the voice of Pelagea Ivanovna. 'Are
you awake?'

'Mm-hmm,' I mumbled, still half asleep.

'I've come to say you needn't hurry over to surgery this
morning. Only two people have come.'

'What? You're joking.'

'No, honestly. There's a blizzard, doctor, a blizzard,' she repeated joyfully through the keyhole. 'And the two who are here have only got decayed teeth. Demyan Lukich will pull them out.'

'Yes, but . . .' Without knowing why, I had already jumped out of bed.

The day turned out splendidly. After doing my round, I spent the rest of the time lounging around my quarters, whistling snatches of opera, smoking, drumming my fingers on the windowpanes. Outside was a sight I had never seen before. There was no sky and no earth – only twisting, swirling whiteness, sideways and aslant, up and down, as though the devil had gone mad with a packet of tooth-powder.

At noon I issued an instruction to Aksinya to boil three buckets and a kettle of water. I had not had a proper wash for a month.

Between us Aksinya and I dragged from the storeroom a washtub of unbelievable dimensions and put it on the kitchen floor. (No question, naturally, of there being any proper bathtubs in our remote spot; the only ones were in the hospital itself – and they were broken.)

By about two o'clock in the afternoon the whirling mesh of snow outside had noticeably thinned out, and I was sitting naked in the washtub with a lathered head.

'Ah, this is more like it . . .' I muttered deliciously as I poured scalding water down my back. 'This is the life! We'll have lunch afterwards and then – bed. And provided I'm allowed a full night's sleep, I don't care if a hundred and fifty people come tomorrow. What's the news, Aksinya?'

Aksinya was in the scullery, waiting till my ablutions were completed.

'The clerk at the Shalometyevo estate is getting married,' Aksinya replied.

'Is he now! So she's accepted him, has she?'

'Of course. He's madly in love . . .' crooned Aksinya, clattering the dishes.

'Is she pretty?'

'Prettiest girl for miles around. Slim, blonde . . .'

'You don't say!'

At that moment there was a hammering at the door. Frowning, I started to rinse myself and listened.

'The doctor's having a bath,' Aksinya sang out, to be answered by a rumbling bass voice.

'A note for you, doctor,' Aksinya squeaked through the key-hole.

'Pass it round the door.'

I clambered out of the bath, shivering and cursing my luck as I took the damp envelope from Aksinya's hand.

'I'm not leaving this tub, that's for sure. After all, I'm only human,' I said without much confidence as I sat down again in the washtub and opened the letter.

Dear Colleague (large exclamation mark). I impl (crossed out) beg you earnestly to come at once. A woman has suffered a blow on the head and is bleeding from the orific . . . (crossed out) from her nose and mouth. She is unconscious. I cannot cope. I earnestly beg you to come. The driver's horses are excellent. Her pulse is poor. Have administered camphor. (Signed) Doctor (illegible).

'Born unlucky,' I thought miserably as I looked at the firewood glowing in the stove.

'Was it a man who brought this?'

'Yes.'

'Ask him to come in here.'

He entered and for a moment I thought he was an ancient Roman from his gleaming helmet planted on top of a fur hat with enormous earflaps. He was enveloped in a wolfskin coat, and I felt the gust of cold as he came in.

'Why are you wearing a helmet?' I enquired, shielding my partly washed body with a towel.

'I'm a fireman from Shalometyevo. We have a fire brigade there . . .' the Roman explained.

'Who is the doctor who wrote this?'

'He came on a visit to the agronomist. Young doctor, he is. It's a terrible business, terrible . . .'

'Who is the woman?'

'The clerk's bride-to-be.'

Aksinya groaned from behind the door.

'What happened?' (I could hear Aksinya sidle up and glue her ear to the door.)

'Yesterday they had an engagement party, and afterwards the clerk wanted to take her for a sleigh-ride. He harnessed up a fast horse, sat her in the sleigh and started off towards the gate. But then the horse broke into a gallop with such a jerk that the girl fell out and hit her forehead on the gatepost. She just sort of flew out. It was the most terrible accident, I can't tell you . . . They had to hold the clerk down to stop him killing himself. He's gone crazy.'

'Look,' I said miserably, 'I'm having a bath. Why couldn't you have brought her here?' So saying I doused my head with water and rinsed the soap into the tub.

'Couldn't be done, sir,' the fireman said in an agonised voice and clasped his hands in entreaty. 'Not a chance, sir. The girl would have died.'

'But how can *we* go? There's a blizzard outside!'

'It's letting up – in fact, sir, it's died down completely. I've a couple of fast horses, harnessed in tandem. We'll be there inside an hour.'

I gave a faint groan, clambered out of the tub, and sluiced myself furiously with two buckets of water. Then, squatting on my haunches in front of the mouth of the stove I made an attempt to dry my hair a little by sticking my head right in.

'I'm bound to end up with pneumonia after a trip like this. In any case, what am I going to do with her? I can tell from his note that this doctor is even less experienced than I am. I know absolutely nothing except the few tips I've managed to pick up in six months' practice, and he knows even less. He's obviously only just qualified. And he thinks I'm an experienced man . . .'

Preoccupied with these thoughts, I was not even aware of getting dressed, which was no simple matter: trousers and shirt, felt boots, over my shirt a leather jerkin, then an overcoat topped by a sheepskin, fur hat, and my bag containing caffeine, camphor, morphine, adrenalin, clamps, sterile dressings, hypodermic, probe, a Browning automatic, cigarettes, matches, watch, stethoscope.

The weather was no longer so alarming, although the daylight was fading and darkness drawing in as we drove through the outskirts of the village. The snowfall seemed to have eased, and was falling diagonally in only one direction against my right cheek. The fireman's bulk completely hid the rear horse's rump from my view. The animals set off at a cracking pace, got into their stride, and the sleigh began flying over the bumpy track. I sank down into the seat and at once started to warm up; I thought of pneumonia and wondered whether a fragment of bone had broken off from inside the girl's skull and penetrated the brain.

'Are these fire brigade horses?' I asked through my sheepskin collar.

'Oh-huh . . . huh . . .' grunted the driver without turning round.

'What has the doctor done to her?'

'Well, sir, he . . . huh . . . trouble is, he's only studied venereal diseases.'

The blizzard moaned through a copse, then lashed out, whistling, as we drove past the shelter of the trees. I felt I was swaying, swaying, swaying . . . until I found myself in the changing-room of Sandunov's steam baths in Moscow – fully dressed, wearing my fur coat, and bathed in sweat. Then a torch flared up, the baths filled with cold water, I opened my eyes and saw a helmet shimmering in a blood-red glow. I thought there was a fire . . . then I blinked and realised that we had arrived. I was outside a white colonnaded building in the neo-classical style of Nicholas I. All around was pitch darkness, I was surrounded by firemen and a flame was flickering above their heads. Thereupon I dragged out my watch through a chink in my fur coat: it was five o'clock. The drive had taken not one hour but two and a half.

'Make sure at once that I have some horses to take me back,' I said.

'Very good,' the driver replied.

Half asleep and feeling as damp under my leather jerkin as though I had been in a hot compress, I went into the hallway. Lamplight struck me from one side, throwing shadows on the varnished floor. A fair-haired young man with a haunted look came running out wearing trousers that had a freshly ironed crease. His white tie with black polka dots was askew, his starched shirt-front had come loose and was bulging out, but his jacket looked fresh from the tailors, brand new, with creases so crisp that they might have been cut out of metal.

The man waved his arms, clutched my fur coat and shook me as he pressed against me, moaning softly:

'Oh, doctor . . . my dear fellow . . . quickly . . . she's dying. I'm a murderer.' He glanced aside, opened his eyes in a wild, tragic stare and said to someone: 'I'm a murderer, that's what I am.'

Then he broke into sobs, clutched at his thin, straggling hair and began pulling at it. I could see from the strands sticking to his fingers that he was literally tearing out his hair.

'Stop it,' I said and pushed his arm aside.

He was led away, and some women came running towards me.

My coat was removed, I was led over gleaming floors and into a room with a white bed. A very young doctor rose from a chair to greet me. His expression was agonised and distraught. For a second I caught a look of astonishment in his eyes as he saw that I was as young as he was. We were, in fact, as alike as two portraits of the same person; we were even the same age. Then he was so overcome with delight at seeing me that he even gulped for breath.

'I'm so glad . . . my dear colleague . . . you see, her pulse is failing. The fact is I'm a venereologist. Thank God you came.'

Lying on a piece of gauze on the table was a hypodermic syringe and several ampoules of yellow oil. The sound of the clerk weeping could be heard through the door, which then closed as the figure of a woman in white materialised at my shoulder. The bedroom was in semi-darkness, a piece of green material having been draped half over the lamp. A face the colour of paper lay on the pillow amid the greenish gloom. The nose had begun to look pinched and sharp, and the nostrils were plugged with cotton wool that was pink with blood.

'Her pulse . . .' the doctor whispered to me.

I took the lifeless arm, applied my fingers with a now habitual gesture and shuddered. I could feel a thin, rapid flutter which broke off and picked up again as a mere faint thread. I felt the customary stab of cold in the pit of my stomach as I always do when I see death face to face. I hate it. I managed to break off the end of a capsule and draw the yellow oil into the syringe, but the injection was only a mechanical gesture and forcing the liquid under the skin of the girl's arm was a waste of time.

Her lower jaw began to twitch as though she were choking, slackened and hung down; the body tensed under the blanket as though hunching with cold, then went limp. And the last trickle of her pulse faded away beneath my fingers.

'She's dead,' I whispered into the doctor's ear.

The white figure with grey hair collapsed on to the smooth blanket and fell across the body, shaking convulsively.

'Hush, hush,' I said softly to the woman in white. The doctor grimaced uneasily towards the door.

'He has been tormenting me,' he said in a very low voice.

Between us we arranged to leave the weeping mother in the bedroom, to tell nothing to anyone else, and to remove the clerk to a distant room. There I said to him:

'If you won't allow us to inject you with a sedative, we can't do anything. You are distracting us and preventing us from working.'

Finally he agreed. Weeping quietly, he took off his jacket, we rolled up the sleeve of the smart new shirt he had bought specially for his engagement party and gave him a morphine injection. The other doctor returned to the dead girl on the pretext of attending to her, while I stayed with the clerk. The morphine worked sooner than I had expected. Within a quarter of an hour his maudlin laments became more and more incoherent, he grew drowsy, then laid his tear-stained face on his arm and fell asleep, oblivious at last to the weeping, the movement, the rustling and muffled sobs around us.

'Look, my dear fellow, it's dangerous to try and go back now. You could easily lose your way,' the doctor whispered to me in the hallway. 'Stay and spend the night here.'

'No, I can't. I must go at all costs. The driver promised that I would be taken back at once.'

'They can certainly take you back, but you must realise . . .'

'I have three typhus patients whom I can't leave. I have to see them every night.'

'Well, if that's the case . . .'

As we stood there in the hall he diluted some spirit with water and gave it to me to drink, which I immediately followed by eating a piece of ham. I felt a warm glow in my stomach and my sense of depression was dulled a little. I went back into the bedroom for a last look at the dead girl, glanced once more at the clerk, left the doctor a capsule of morphine, wrapped myself up and went out on to the porch.

The horses stood hanging their heads as the storm whistled and snow lashed at their flanks. A torch flickered.

'Do you know the way?' I enquired as I wound a muffler across my mouth.

'We know the way all right,' the driver replied gloomily (he was no longer wearing his helmet), 'but you ought to stop here for the night . . .'

The very earflaps of his hat told me that he would almost rather die than go.

'You ought to stay, sir,' added another man, who was holding the guttering torch. 'It's bad out there.'

'Eight miles . . .' I grumbled. 'We'll make it. I have patients who are seriously ill . . .' And I climbed into the sleigh.

I confess I omitted to say that the mere thought of staying in that house of misfortune, where I was impotent and useless, was intolerable.

Hopelessly, the coachman sat down heavily on the driver's seat, straightened up and gave a jerk as we moved off through the gateway at a smart pace. The torch went out as though it had vanished or been doused. A minute later, though, something else caught my attention: turning round with difficulty, I noticed that not only was the torch no more to be seen but Shalometyevo itself and all its buildings had disappeared as if in a dream. This gave me an unpleasant shock.

'That's pretty odd,' I half-thought, half-mumbled to myself. I stuck my nose out for a moment, but the weather was so terrible that I stuck it in again. The whole world had been rolled into one bundle that was being buffeted in every direction at once.

For a moment I wondered whether to turn back, but I rejected the idea, burrowed deeper into the hay at the bottom of the sledge as though in a boat, hunched myself up and closed my eyes. At once the scrap of green material on the lamp and a white face floated before my inner eye, immediately followed by a flash of realisation: 'It's a fracture of the base of the skull . . . Yes, of course . . . that's it!' In a burst of confidence I felt that this must be the correct diagnosis. A brainwave –but what good was it? It was as useless now as it would have been earlier; there was nothing to be done about it. What a ghastly thing to happen! What absurdly precarious lives we lead! What must be happening now in that house? It was too sickening even to contemplate. Then I began to feel sorry for myself: mine was a hard life. Everyone else was asleep now, their stoves a-glow, and once more I had been prevented from taking a proper bath. The blizzard was tossing me about like a leaf. Even when I did reach home, the chances were that I would be called out somewhere else. Or I would catch pneumonia and die out here . . . In this mood of self-pity I sank into the dark of oblivion, though I have no idea how long I spent in that state: this time I did not dream of being in a bath-house, because I was too cold. And it grew colder and colder.

When I opened my eyes a black back loomed in front of me, and I realised that we were not moving any longer.

'Have we arrived?' I asked, blinking as I gazed blearily around me.

The black-coated driver shifted gloomily in his seat, then suddenly jumped down, and I had the impression that he was being whirled around. Without a trace of deference he said:

'No we haven't . . . ought to listen to what people say . . . What did I tell you? It'll be the death of us and the horses too.'

'Don't tell me you've lost the road?' A cold shiver went down my spine.

'Road? What road?' the driver echoed in a despairing voice. 'The road might be anywhere for all I can see now. There's not a sign of it . . . We've been driving for four hours, but God knows where we've been going. That's what comes of . . .'

Four hours. I stirred myself, felt for my watch and extracted my matches. Why did I bother? It was useless; not one match would light. I struck them, they sparked and were instantly blown out.

'Four hours, I tell you,' said the driver in a funereal voice. 'What are we going to do now?'

'Where are we?'

The question was so stupid that the driver did not even feel obliged to reply. He turned to peer in various directions, and there were moments when I felt that he was standing still and the sleigh was swivelling round with me in it. I clambered out, to discover at once that I sank into snow up to my knees right beside the sleigh-runner. The rear horse was stuck up to its belly in a snowdrift, its mane hanging down to one side like a woman who has let down her hair.

'Did the horses stop of their own accord?'

'Yes. The wretched beasts are worn out.'

I suddenly remembered a short story I had read and for some reason felt a burst of resentment at Leo Tolstoy.

'It was all right for him, living comfortably at Yasnaya Polyana,' I thought, 'I bet he was never called out to people who were dying . . .'

I felt sorry for the fireman and myself. Then came another stab of wild fear, which I suppressed.

'Don't be a coward,' I muttered to myself through clenched teeth.

At once came a surge of fiery energy.

'Look,' I said, feeling my teeth freeze as I spoke, 'we mustn't let ourselves get despondent in a situation like this, or we really shall be done for. The horses have had a bit of a rest by now, and we must get on the move again. You go on ahead, get hold of the lead horse by the bridle and I'll drive. Unless we get out of this drift we'll be snowed up.'

Despite the utter dejection signalled by his earflaps, the driver floundered forward. Stumbling and falling, he made his way to the lead horse. Getting ourselves out of that drift seemed interminable. The figure of the driver was blotted from sight as the dry, stinging snow drove into my eyes.

'Giddap!' groaned the driver.

'Giddap! Giddap!' I shouted, slapping at the horses with the reins.

Little by little the horses dragged themselves forward, churning up the snow. The sleigh began to rock like a boat at sea. The driver seemed to shrink and then to grow again as he struggled painfully ahead.

For about a quarter of an hour we moved in this fashion, until I began at last to feel from the creak of the runners that we were on more even ground. With a surge of joy I noticed the steady flicker of the horses' hind hooves as they broke into a trot.

'The snow's thinner here – we must be back on the road!' I shouted.

'Uh-huh,' replied the driver. He stumbled back towards me and straightened up to his full height.

'Seems like it's the road,' the fireman boomed, so excited that there was even a slight tremor in his voice. 'As long as we don't lose it again. Let's hope for the best . . .'

We resumed our places. The horses began moving faster. The blizzard slackened and seemed to shrink. But above and all around there was still nothing but murk. I had already lost hope of reaching the hospital. I just wanted to arrive somewhere – after all, a road must lead to some kind of habitation.

Suddenly the horses gave a jerk and quickened their gait. I was delighted, not knowing the reason for it.

'Perhaps they've sensed we're near a village?' I asked.

The driver did not reply. I stood up in the sleigh and began to peer about me. A strange sound, at once plaintive and menacing, arose somewhere in the dark but quickly died away. An uneasy feeling came over me and I was reminded of the thin whine uttered by the clerk as he had laid his head on his arms. Suddenly to my right I made out a dark blob which grew until it looked like a black cat, grew bigger still and came nearer. The fireman swung round to face me, I noticed that his jaw was quivering and he said:

'Did you see them, doctor?'

One horse started tugging to the right, the other to the left, for a second the fireman fell back on to my knees, groaned, pulled himself upright again, leaned forward and began lashing with the reins. The horses snorted and picked up speed, kicking up lumps of snow behind them but quivering and moving unevenly.

Several times in succession a shudder went through my body. As I pulled myself up, thrust a hand under my coat and drew out my automatic I cursed myself for having left the spare magazine at home. Since I had refused to spend the night at Shalometyevo, why in hell hadn't I had the sense to bring a torch with me? I had a mental vision of a brief report in the newspaper about myself and the unfortunate fireman.

The cat grew to the size of a dog, running a short distance away from the sleigh. I turned round and saw, even nearer to us, a second four-legged beast. I swear that it had pointed ears and was loping along behind the sleigh as easily as across a smooth parquet floor. There was something insolent and threatening about their persistence. 'Is it a pack or are they only two?' I wondered, and at the word 'pack' I felt doused in a wave of heat beneath my fur coat and even my toes ceased to feel cold.

'Hold tight and stop for a moment, I'm going to shoot,' I announced in a voice that I did not recognise as my own.

In reply the driver only groaned and drew his head into his shoulders. There was a flash and a deafening report, then a second and a third. After that I cannot remember how long I was tossed about on the floor of the sleigh. I could hear the wild, shrill snorting of the horses, I clutched the pistol, hit my head on something, tried to wriggle out of the hay. In mortal fear I imagined a huge, sinewy body suddenly landing on my chest. Mentally I could already see my own lacerated entrails . . .

At that moment the driver howled:

'Hey – there it is . . . oh Lord, only a little further . . .'

Finally I succeeded in overcoming the embrace of the heavy sheepskin, freed my hands and pulled myself up. Behind and to

either side there were no more black beasts. The snowfall was
now thinner and quite tolerable, and through the thin veil
flickered a gleaming eye, an entrancing eye which I would have
recognised from a thousand and which I can see to this day: the
light of my hospital. The dark mass of the building loomed
behind it. 'Home, sweet home . . .' I thought, and suddenly in
ecstasy I fired another two shots from the automatic towards
where the wolves had vanished.

The fireman was standing half way up the staircase leading from
the lower half of the curious two-storey layout of the doctor's
flat; I was at the top of the staircase, Aksinya at the bottom
wearing a sheepskin jerkin.

'Even if you gave me a gold medal,' said the driver, 'I wouldn't
make that journey again . . .' He did not finish, but downed a
glass of neat spirit at one gulp. Then wheezing horribly he turned
to Aksinya and added, stretching his arms as wide as his build
would allow: 'Big as that, they were . . .'

'Did she die? You couldn't save her?' Aksinya asked.

'Yes, she died,' I replied indifferently.

A quarter of an hour later all was silent. The light went out
downstairs. I was alone upstairs. For some reason I gave a
convulsive laugh, unbuttoned my shirt, then buttoned it up
again, went to the bookcase and took out a manual of surgery,
started to look up something about fractures of the base of the
skull, threw the book aside.

When I had undressed and crept under the bedclothes, within
half a minute a fit of shivering overcame me; then it stopped and
warmth flooded all through my body.

'Even if you gave me a gold medal . . .' I mumbled as I began
to doze. 'I wouldn't go again . . .'

'You'll go, you'll go,' said the blizzard in a mocking howl. It
roared over the roof, then boomed in the chimney, flew out
again, rustled past the window, vanished.

'You'll go, go, go, go,' ticked the clock, but the sound was
growing duller.

No more. Silence. Sleep.

The Vanishing Eye

So a year has passed. It is exactly a year since I first drove up to this house. Then as now a veil of rain shrouded the windows and the last leaves drooped forlornly on the birch trees. All around, nothing seems to have changed. But I have changed a great deal. I shall celebrate the anniversary alone with my memories.

I cross the creaking floor of my bedroom and look into the mirror. Yes, the difference is enormous. A year ago this mirror, just unpacked from my trunk, reflected a shaven face. My twenty-four-year-old head was adorned with a parting. Now the parting has gone, my hair is brushed unceremoniously straight back. Who is there to impress with a neat parting anyway, when you are twenty miles from the railway line? The same has happened to my shaving: my upper lip now wears a solid growth rather like a harsh yellow toothbrush; my cheeks feel like a cheese-grater, so that if my forearm happens to start itching while I am at work I get relief by rubbing it against my cheek. It always gets like that when I shave only once a week instead of three times.

I once read somewhere – I forget where – about an Englishman who was cast away on a desert island. He was an interesting case. He was stranded on that island for so long that he suffered from hallucinations, and when a ship passed the island and a boatload of men came ashore to his rescue, he – the castaway – greeted them with a volley of revolver shots, being convinced that they were a mirage, an illusion produced by the vast, empty expanse of water. Yet he was clean shaven. He had shaved every day on a desert island. I remember the profound respect I felt for that proud son of Britannia. When I arrived here my luggage, too, contained a Gillette safety razor with a dozen blades, as well as a cut-throat razor and a shaving brush. And I finally determined to shave every other day, because this place was no better than a desert island.

But one bright April day, when I had laid out all these English treasures in the slanting, golden sunlight and had just shaved my right cheek to gleaming smoothness, in burst Yegorich, the watchman, his torn old boots clattering like a horse's hooves, to report that a woman was giving birth in the bushes beside a stream in the nature reserve. I remember wiping my left cheek with a towel and flying out of the house with Yegorich. Three of us then ran to the stream, turbulent and swollen between fiery clumps of willow – the midwife with a pair of forceps, a roll of bandage and a bottle of iodine, myself with eyes popping out of my head, and Yegorich bringing up the rear. Every fifth pace or so he squatted down on the ground and swore as he tugged at his left boot: the sole had torn loose. The wind flew towards us, the sweet, wild wind of the Russian spring, the comb had fallen out of Pelagea Ivanovna's hair, her knot of hair unwound itself and flapped against her shoulder.

'Why the hell do you spend all your money on drink?' I muttered to Yegorich as we ran. 'It's a disgrace. You're a hospital watchman and you go around barefoot.'

'What d'you expect on my pay?' Yegorich grumbled irritably. 'Twenty roubles a month and I'm supposed to sweat my guts out . . . Oh, damn the thing!' He stamped his foot on the ground like an evil-tempered horse. 'Can't even keep body and soul together on the money I get, let alone buy a decent pair of boots.'

'It all goes on drink with you,' I panted breathlessly, 'and that's why you look like a tramp.'

From the little rotting bridge came a faint, pathetic cry which was carried across the rushing stream and faded away. As we ran up we saw a dishevelled woman, her face contorted into a grimace. Her headscarf had slipped off, her hair was clinging to her sweating forehead, she was rolling her eyes in pain and clawing at her sheepskin jerkin with her nails. Bright, fresh blood had stained the first thin, pale blades of grass which were just beginning to sprout on the muddy, waterlogged soil.

'She didn't make it in time, the poor thing,' Pelagea Ivanovna said hurriedly as she unrolled the bandage, looking like a witch with her wild, floating hair.

And there, to the cheerful sound of roaring water as it swirled past the blackened timber supports of the bridge, Pelagea Ivanovna and I delivered a baby of the male sex. We delivered him alive and saved the mother. Then two nurses and Yegorich, his left foot bare after he had finally cast off the detested, torn sole, carried the mother back to the hospital on a stretcher.

Later, when she lay calm and pale under the bedclothes, when the baby had been put beside her in a cot and all was in order, I asked her:

'Couldn't you have found a better place than that bridge to have your baby, my dear? Why didn't you come here on horseback?'

She replied:

'My father-in-law wouldn't give me a horse. It's only three miles, he said, you'll easily get there on your own. You're a healthy woman. No point in tiring a horse for nothing . . .'

'Your father-in-law's a fool and a swine,' I retorted.

'Oh, what benighted people these are,' Pelagea Ivanovna added pityingly, and then giggled at something.

I caught her look, which was fixed on my left cheek.

I went out and glanced at the mirror in the labour ward. The mirror showed what it usually showed: a warped physiognomy of clearly degenerate type with an apparently blackened left eye. But – and here the mirror was not to blame – the right cheek of this degenerate was as smooth as a dance-floor, while the left was covered by a dense, reddish growth. The chin formed the dividing line. I recalled a book in a yellow binding entitled *The Penal Colony of Sakhalin*, which contained photographs of various criminal types.

'Murder, housebreaking, a bloodstained axe . . .' I thought, 'ten years' hard . . . Yes, it's a pretty weird life here on my desert island. I must go and finish shaving.'

Breathing the scent of April borne in from the dark ploughland, I listened to the rooks cawing in the tops of the birch trees, squinted in the spring sunlight and walked across the courtyard to complete my shave. That was about three o'clock in the afternoon. I finished shaving at nine o'clock that night. At Muryovo surprises like childbirth in the bushes, I have observed, never come singly. No sooner had I grasped the door handle on my porch then a horse's muzzle appeared in the main gateway and a heavily mud-spattered cart rumbled in behind it. It was driven by a peasant woman, who shouted in a thin voice:

'Whoa there, you devil!'

From the porch I could hear the whimpering of a little boy coming from a bundle of rags.

Of course he turned out to have a broken leg, and the *feldsher* and I worked for two hours setting the little boy's leg in plaster, during which the child howled without cease. After that it was supper time, then I felt too lazy to shave and wanted to do some reading instead; after which twilight had begun to set in and the far distance grew blurred as I finished shaving, frowning miserably. But because the serrated Gillette had lain forgotten in the soapy water, it acquired a permanent little strip of rust as a memorial to that childbirth by the bridge in springtime.

There was really no point in shaving twice a week. At times we were completely snowed up, once there was an unearthly blizzard when we were imprisoned for two days in the Muryovo hospital without even sending anyone the six miles to Voznesensk to fetch newspapers; for many a long evening I paced up and down the length of my study, longing for newspapers with the same hunger that in childhood I had longed for Fenimore Cooper's *The Deerslayer*. Even so, English customs were not wholly extinguished on the desert island of Muryovo, and from time to time I would take my gleaming toy out of its black case and languidly shave myself, emerging as smooth and clean as any proud member of the Island Race. It was only a pity that there was no one to admire me.

Oh yes, there was another occasion when, as I remember, I had taken out my razor and Aksinya had just brought a chipped jug of hot water into my study; at that moment there was a thunderous knocking at the door and I was called out. Pelagea Ivanovna and I set off into the terrifying distance, wrapped in sheepskin coats, and like a black phantom formed by the shape of the horses, the driver and ourselves, we struggled through the wild, white ocean. The blizzard whistled, howled, spat and screamed with laughter like a witch, everything was blotted from sight and I felt a familiar cold stab in the region of the solar plexus at the thought that we might lose our way in this diabolical, swirling haze and all perish: Pelagea Ivanovna, the driver, the horses and myself. I remember, too, having the idiotic notion that when we began to freeze to death and were half buried in snow, I would inject the midwife, myself and the driver with morphia . . . What for? . . . Well, to lessen the agony . . . 'You will die of cold quite well enough, physician, without morphia,' I remember the dry voice of common sense saying to me in reply, 'so don't bother . . .' Ah-aahh! Ss-sss . . . ! screeched the witch, as we were flung from side to side in the sleigh. Well, somewhere on the back page of a Moscow newspaper there would be a report of how Doctor So-and-So, Pelagea Ivanovna, a driver and a pair of horses had perished from the 'rigours of the service'. Peace to their ashes, out there in the sea of snow. Dear me, what rubbish creeps into one's head when called out on a journey in the so-called line of duty.

We did not perish, nor did we lose our way but reached the village of Grishchevo, where I set about performing the second podalic version of my career. The mother was the wife of the village schoolmaster, and while by the light of a lamp Pelagea Ivanovna and I struggled with the version, blood up to our elbows and sweat streaming into our eyes, through the plank door we could hear the husband moaning and pacing up and down in the back regions of the cottage. To the sound of his unbroken sobbing and the woman's groans I managed, if the truth be known, to break the baby's arm. The child was born dead. God, how the sweat ran down my back! For an instant I somehow imagined that some huge, grim, black figure would appear and burst into the cottage, saying in a stony voice: 'Aha! Take away his degree!'

Exhausted, I gazed at the little yellow corpse and the wax-like mother lying motionless under anaesthesia. Snow-laden air streamed in through the small upper window, which we had opened for a moment to disperse the stifling reek of chloroform, and the stream of air was being transformed into a cloud of steam. Then I slammed the pane shut and turned again to stare at the helplessly dangling little arm cradled in the midwife's embrace. I cannot describe the state of desperation in which I returned home – alone, as I had left Pelagea Ivanovna to take care of the mother. As I was rocked about on the sleigh journey through the dwindling snowstorm, the grim forest stared at me in hopeless, reproachful despair. I felt beaten, crushed, smothered by a cruel fate which had flung me into this wilderness to struggle single-handed, devoid of support or advice.

I had been made to suffer unbelievable rigours. No matter how delicate or complex the case – usually surgical – I had had to set my unshaven face squarely to it and conquer it. And if I failed, as now, then I was not only flung from bump to bump but tormented by the thought of the dead baby and the mother I had left behind. Next day, as soon as the snowstorm abated, Pelagea Ivanovna would bring her to the hospital, and then the big question would be whether I managed to pull her through. But *how* was I to pull her through? For the fact was that my methods were purely hit and miss: I was hopelessly ignorant. Up till now I had been lucky and had successfully pulled off some incredible things; but today my luck had run out. I felt my heart gripped by loneliness, by cold, by awareness of my utter isolation. What was more, by breaking the baby's arm I might have actually committed a crime. I felt like driving off somewhere to cast myself at someone's feet and confess that I, Doctor So-and-So, had broken a child's arm – take away my degree, dear colleagues, I am unworthy of it, send me to Sakhalin! God, how neurotic I felt!

I slumped to the bottom of the sleigh and huddled up to stop the cold from devouring me quite so ferociously, and felt like a wretched little puppy, homeless and clumsy.

We drove and drove for hours, until the light over the hospital gateway, small but so cheering and welcoming, came in sight. It flickered, vanished, flared up, disappeared again, then beckoned once more. The sight of it eased my desolation a little, and when the light at last shone firmly before my eyes, when it grew bigger and closer, when the hospital walls changed from black to whitish and I drove through the gateway, I was already saying to myself:

'The arm doesn't matter. The baby was already dead when you broke it. Don't think about the arm; remember that the mother's alive.'

The lantern and the familiar porch cheered me up somewhat; but even so, once indoors and climbing the stairs to my study, feeling the heat from the stove and savouring in advance the healing oblivion of sleep, I mumbled to myself:

'That may be so, but the loneliness is terrible here. Terrible.'

The razor lay on the table, beside it a jug of once-hot water. I threw the razor contemptuously into a drawer. And I was badly in need of a shave . . .

And now a whole year has passed. While it lasted it seemed endlessly varied, multifarious, complex and terrible, although I now realise that it has flown by like a hurricane. I stare into the mirror and see the traces that it has left on my face. There is more severity and anxiety in my eyes, the mouth is more confident and manly, while the vertical wrinkle between my eyebrows will remain for a lifetime – as long, in fact, as my memories. I can see them as I look in the mirror, chasing each other in headlong succession.

In the days when I was still worried by the thought that I might lose my medical degree, I imagined some fantastic tribunal calling me to account and fearsome judges asking me:

'What about the soldier's jaw? Answer, miserable graduate!'

I am never likely to forget it. It all happened because although Demyan Lukich could draw teeth as handily as a carpenter pulling rusty nails out of old timber, tact and a sense of my own dignity told me that one of the first things I should do at Muryovo hospital was to learn to extract teeth myself. Demyan Lukich might be absent or sick; our midwives could do anything, with one exception – they would not pull teeth out; it was not their job.

And so . . . I well remember the red-cheeked but suffering face of the man sitting in front of me on a stool. He was a soldier, one of the many who had returned home from the disintegrating front line after the revolution. I recall equally well the massive, powerful but carious tooth, solidly rooted in the jaw. Frowning in an effort to look as if I knew what I was doing and grunting with effort, I clamped the pincers on the tooth, vividly recalling as I did so Chekhov's famous short story about a sexton having his tooth pulled. Suddenly, for the first time, that story did not seem funny at all. There was a loud crunching noise from the soldier's mouth and he gave a short yelp:

'Oo-ow!'

After that I felt no more resistance and the pincers jerked out of his mouth gripping a white, bloodstained object. At the sight of it my heart missed a beat, because this object exceeded any tooth in size, even a soldier's molar. At first I could not understand it, then I almost burst into tears: although the jaws of the pincers held a tooth with a very long root, there was also dangling from the tooth an enormous, jagged piece of gleaming white bone.

'I've broken his jaw . . .' I thought, and my legs went weak. With a prayer of thanks to fate that neither the *feldsher* nor the midwives were watching me, I furtively wrapped the fruit of my over-enthusiastic labours in a piece of gauze and hid it in my pocket. Swaying on his stool, the soldier was clutching the leg of the gynaecological chair with one hand and a leg of the stool with the other as he stared at me wildly, his eyes starting out of his head. In some confusion I handed him a glass with a solution of potassium permanganate and said:

'Rinse.'

It was a stupid thing to do. He took a mouthful of the solution, but when he spat it out into the bowl, it came out mixed with the soldier's crimson blood as a dense liquid of indescribable colour. At once blood began spurting out of his mouth so fast that I froze with horror. If I had slit the wretched man's throat with a razor, I doubt if he would have bled harder. Pushing aside the glass of permanganate I flung myself at the soldier with pads of gauze and plugged the gaping hole in his jaw. The gauze instantly turned red, and as I took it out I was appalled to see that the hole was big enough for a large greengage to have fitted into it with room to spare.

'I've sent this soldier to glory,' I thought despairingly as I tugged long strips of gauze out of the jar. At last the bleeding stopped and I painted the hole in his jaw with iodine.

'Don't eat anything for the next three hours,' I said to my patient in a shaky voice.

'Thank you very much, sir,' the soldier replied, staring with some amazement at the bowl full of his blood.

'Er, look . . .' I said miserably, 'I tell you what . . . you'd better come and see me again tomorrow or the day after. I, er . . . well, I shall have to take another look . . . You have another tooth alongside which looks suspicious. All right?'

'Thanks very much,' the soldier replied sullenly as he went out clutching his cheek. I staggered into the waiting room and sat there for a while, clasping my head and rocking back and forth as though myself suffering from toothache. About five times I pulled the hard, bloodstained lump out of my pocket and put it back again.

For a week I lived in a fog, grew thin and sickly.

'The soldier will get gangrene, blood-poisoning . . . God, why did I have to use the pincers on him?'

Absurd visions floated before my mind's eye. The soldier is beginning to shiver. For a while he is well enough, he walks about, talks about Kerensky and life in the front line; then he talks less and less. Soon he no longer wants to talk about Kerensky. Now he is lying on a cotton pillow and he is delirious. He has a temperature of 104°. The whole village calls to see him. Finally, his nose growing sharper, he is laid out on the table with an ikon on his chest.

The villagers start gossiping.

'What did he die from?'

'That doctor pulled his tooth out.'

'Ah, so that was it, was it?'

And so the talk goes on. There is an enquiry. A stern man comes:

'Did you extract the soldier's tooth?'

'Yes . . . I did.'

The soldier is exhumed. A trial. Disgrace. I am the cause of his death. And I am no longer a doctor, but a wretched outcast, worse – an unperson.

The soldier did not come back, and my misery increased as the gauze-wrapped lump in my desk drawer dried and turned the colour of rust. Within a week I would have to go into town to fetch my staff's pay. I went after five days, and made my way straight to a doctor in the district hospital. He was a man with a little nicotine-stained beard who had worked there for twenty-five years; he had seen a great deal in his time. I sat that evening in his study, dejectedly sipping lemon tea and fidgeting with the tablecloth. At last I could hold out no longer, and with much beating about the bush I made up a vague, spurious story about how I had heard of cases . . . if one extracted a tooth . . . broke the jaw . . . gangrene could result, couldn't it? Well, a piece of bone . . . I had read somewhere . . .

He listened and listened, staring at me with faded eyes from under his shaggy eyebrows and then suddenly he said:

'You broke off the tooth-socket . . . Don't worry, you'll make a fine tooth-puller in time . . . Forget the tea, let's go and have some vodka before dinner.'

And at once the tormenting vision of that soldier vanished from my mind forever.

Ah, those memories in the mirror. A whole year of them. How I laugh now when I think about that tooth-socket! Of course, I shall never be able to draw teeth the way Demyan Lukich does. After all, he extracts about five a day while I do about one a fortnight. Even so, I can pull them well enough to be the envy of many doctors; I don't break the socket any more, and if I did I would not lose my head.

But teeth are nothing compared with all the things I saw and did in that year of unique experience.

Evening was seeping into my room. The lamp was already lit and as I floated in an acrid haze of tobacco smoke totting up my achievements, my heart overflowed with pride. I had done two amputations at the hip, and I had lost count of all the fingers. There were eighteen curettages listed, a hernia and a tracheotomy, all of them successful. And the number of gigantic abscesses I had lanced, not to mention broken limbs set in plaster or starch. I had corrected dislocations. Intubations. Childbirth. Whatever they come with, I've dealt with it. Admittedly I won't undertake a caesarian section; I send them into town for that. But forceps, versions – any number.

When I was sitting the forensic medicine paper of my finals, I remember the professor saying:

'Describe gunshot wounds inflicted at point-blank range.'

I launched into a long and woolly description, during which a page of a very thick textbook floated in my visual memory. At last I ran out of steam, the professor gave me a look of disgust and said in a grating voice:

'Nothing resembling what you have described is to be found in point-blank wounds. How many "fives"* have you been given so far?'

'Fifteen,' I replied.

He put a 'three' against my name and I went out of the room covered in disgrace.

On qualifying, I was soon posted to Muryovo and now I am alone here. The devil alone knows what the characteristics of point-blank wounds are supposed to be, but when I was faced with a man lying on my operating table with a bubbly foam, pink with blood, oozing over his lips, did I lose my head? I did not, even though his chest had been peppered with buckshot at point-blank range, one lung was visible and the flesh of his chest hung in shreds. Six weeks later he left my hospital alive. At university I was not once permitted to hold a pair of obstetrical forceps, yet here – trembling, I admit – I applied them in a moment. I must confess that one baby I delivered looked rather

*Russian examinations, which are generally oral, are marked on a scale of 1 to 5. '5' indicates 'distinction', '4' is 'good', '3' is usually a bare pass.

odd: half of its head was swollen, bluish-purple and without an eye. I turned cold, dimly hearing Pelagea Ivanovna as she said consolingly:

'It's all right, doctor, you've just put one half of the forceps over his eye.'

I shivered with anxiety for two days, but after that the head returned to normal.

And the wounds I have stitched – the cases of suppurating pleurisy when I have had to prise the ribs apart; the cases of pneumonia, typhus, cancer, syphilis, hernia (successfully treated), haemorrhoids, sarcoma.

In a moment of inspiration I opened the out-patients' register and spent an hour analysing and totalling. In a year, up to the very hour of that evening, I had seen 15,613 patients; 200 in-patients had been admitted, of whom only six died.

I closed the book and tottered to bed. At twenty-five years old and celebrating my first professional anniversary, I lay in bed and thought as I fell asleep that I was now vastly experienced. What had I to fear? Nothing. I had extracted peas lodged in little boys' ears, I had wielded the knife countless times . . . My hand had acquired courage and did not shake. I spotted all tricky complications and had acquired a unique ability to under-stand the things that peasant women say. I was able to interpret them like Sherlock Holmes deciphering mysterious documents. Sleep is creeping up on me.

'I cannot,' I mumbled, growing sleepier, 'honestly imagine being brought a case that would floor me . . . perhaps in Moscow they might accuse me of a "*feldsher*" attitude to medicine . . . well, let them . . . it's all right for them in their clinics and teaching hospitals, X-ray cabinets and so on . . . whereas here there's just me . . . peasants couldn't live without me . . . How I used to shudder whenever there was a knock at the door, how I winced with fear . . . Now, though . . .'

'When did it happen?'

'Last week, sir . . . It all swelled up.'

And the woman began to whimper.

It was a grey October morning, the first day of my second year. Yesterday evening I had been congratulating myself, and now this morning I was standing there in my white coat nonplussed.

She was holding a year-old baby in her arms like a log, and the infant had no left eye. In place of an eye there protruded between taught, overstretched eyelids a yellow-coloured ball the size of a small egg. The baby was struggling and crying in pain, the woman snivelling. And I was at a loss.

I looked at it from every possible angle. Demyan Lukich and the midwife were standing behind me in silence; they had never seen anything like it.

'What on earth is it? Cerebral hernia? . . . Hmm . . . well, at least he's alive . . . Sarcoma? No, rather too soft . . . Some revolting, unknown kind of tumour. How could it have developed . . . from an empty eye socket? Perhaps there never was an eye . . . at any rate, there isn't now.'

'Look here,' I said in a burst of inspiration, 'we shall have to cut this thing out.'

I had a mental picture of how I would cut the lower lid, move it to one side and . . . and what? What then? Perhaps it really is part of the brain . . . Ugh, it's soft enough . . . feels like brain.

'What, cut him open?' the peasant woman asked, turning pale. 'Cut his eye? I won't consent.' Horrified, she began wrapping the infant in his rags.

'He has no eye,' I replied categorically. 'Just take a look at where his eye ought to be. Your baby has a strange sort of swelling.'

'Give him some drops, then,' said the woman fearfully.

'You're joking! What sort of drops? No drops are going to do him any good!'

'You wouldn't leave him without an eye, would you?'

'But he *has* no eye, I tell you.'

'He had one the day before yesterday!' the woman exclaimed in desperation. (God!)

'Well, if you say so, then I suppose . . . hell . . . only he hasn't got one now, has he? In any case, my dear, you'd better take the child into town. Right away, so they can operate . . . Don't you agree, Demyan Lukich?'

'M'yes,' the *feldsher* replied gravely, obviously not knowing what to say, 'I've never seen the like of it.'

'Take him to be cut open in town?' the woman cried in horror. 'I won't let you.'

In the end the woman took her baby away without giving us permission to touch the eye. For two days I racked my brains.

shrugged my shoulders and ferreted about in the library in search of illustrations showing babies with protuberant swellings in place of their eyes . . . hopeless.

Then I forgot about the child altogether.

A week passed.

'Anna Zhukhova!' I shouted. In came a cheerful peasant woman carrying a baby.

'What's the trouble?' I enquired mechanically.

'All's well, he's not going to die,' the woman announced with a sarcastic grin. The sound of her voice made me sit up with a jerk.

'Recognise him?' she asked mockingly.

'Wait a moment . . . that's . . . wait a moment – is that the child who . . . ?'

'That's him. Remember you said he had no eye, doctor, and you'd have to cut him open to . . .'

I felt I was going off my head. The woman stared at me triumphantly, her eyes laughing. The baby lay in her arms gazing out at the world with brown eyes. Of the yellow tumour there was no sign.

'This is witchcraft,' I thought weakly. When I had somewhat recovered my wits, I cautiously drew down the eyelid. The baby whimpered and tried to turn his head, but I was still able to see it: a tiny little scar on the mucous membrane . . . Aha!

'As we were driving away from here, it burst.'

'No need to tell me,' I said with embarrassment. 'I see what it was now.'

'And you said he had no eye. Well, it grew again, didn't it?' And the woman giggled, taunting me.

'I see now, damn it . . . An enormous abscess developed under his lower lid, swelled and completely covered the eye . . . Then when it burst, the pus ran out and everything went back into place.'

No, even when I'm on the verge of sleep I shall never again boast that nothing can surprise me. Now that this year is past, the next year will be just as full of surprises as the first. One never stops learning.

Morphine

Clever people have long been aware that happiness is like good health: when you have it, you don't notice it. But as the years go by, oh, the memories, the memories of happiness past!

For myself I realise now that I was happy in that winter of 1917, that headlong, never-to-be-forgotten year of storm and blizzard.

The first blast of the snowstorm snatched me up like a scrap of torn newspaper and transported me from a practice in the depths of the countryside to the town. What, you may wonder, is so special about a country town? If like me you have ever spent the winters snowbound and the summers deep in a landscape of sparse, monotonous woodland, without a single day off in more than a year; if you have ever torn the wrapper off last week's newspaper with your heart beating as though you were a lover joyfully ripping open a pale blue envelope; if you have ever driven twelve miles in a tandem-harnessed sleigh to a woman in labour, then you may realise what the town meant to me.

Kerosene lamps may be very cosy, but I prefer electricity.

And there they were again at last, those seductive little electric lights! The main street of the little town, the snow well flattened by the runners of peasants' sleighs, was hung with red flags and shop signs that entranced the eye: a boot; a golden pretzel; a picture of a young man with insolent, pig-like eyes and a wholly unnatural haircut, signifying that behind those glass doors was the local Figaro, who for thirty kopecks was prepared to shave you at any hour of the day – except on holidays, in which this land of ours abounds.

To this day I shudder when I recall that Figaro's towels, which reminded me forcibly of a page in my German textbook of skin diseases, illustrating with appalling clarity a growth of hard chancre on a man's chin.

But even those towels cannot spoil my happy memories!

At the crossroads stood a real, live policeman, in a dusty shop window one could just make out tin trays packed with rows of cakes topped with orange cream. The square was carpeted with fresh straw, people were driving, walking about and chatting; there was a kiosk selling yesterday's Moscow papers full of thrilling news, and from not far away came the sound of Moscow-bound trains hooting to one another. In short, this was civilisation, Babylon, the Nevsky Prospekt.

The hospital, I need hardly add, boasted separate surgical, medical, isolation and maternity departments. There was an operating theatre with a gleaming autoclave, plated taps and operating tables with ingeniously designed flaps, cogwheels and screws. It had a Medical Superintendent, three interns (beside myself), several *feldshers*, midwives, nurses, a dispensary and a laboratory. Just think – a laboratory, complete with a Zeiss microscope and a fine assortment of stains.

All this impressed me so much that I would shudder and turn cold. It took me several days to get used to it when, in the December twilight, the hospital's single-storey wards would blaze with electric light as though at a word of command.

I was dazzled. Water splashed and roared in the bathtubs, and worn wooden-cased thermometers plunged or floated in them. All day long the children's isolation ward reverberated with moans, thin plaintive weeping and hoarse gurgles. Nurses darted to and fro.

I had shed a heavy burden. I no longer bore the godlike responsibility for everything that happened in the world. It was not my fault if someone developed a strangulated hernia, and I did not shudder when a sleigh drove up bringing a woman with a transverse foetus, a case of epyema requiring operation was no longer my affair. For the first time I felt that there was a limit to my responsibilities. Childbirth? Over there, please, to that low building – the furthest window with the net curtains; there you'll find our obstetrician, a charming, fat, balding man with a ginger moustache. That's his business. The sleigh makes for the curtained window. A compound fracture? You want our chief

surgeon. Inflammation of the lungs? Go and see Pavel Vladimir-
ovich in the medical department.

Oh, what a splendid thing a large hospital is, with its smooth,
well-oiled machinery! I fitted into the mechanism like a new screw
dropping into its appointed slot and took over the children's
department; from then on my days were wholly taken up with
diphtheria and scarlet fever. But only my days. I started sleeping
at night, undisturbed by that ominous nocturnal tapping downstairs, which meant that I was likely to be roused and dragged out
into the darkness to face danger or whatever fate had in store. I
took to reading in the evenings (chiefly about diphtheria and
scarlet fever, but I also developed an odd addiction to Fenimore
Cooper). I appreciated to the full the electric light over my desk,
the charred ash that dropped down on to the tray of my samovar,
my cooling tea, and the chance to sleep after many sleepless
months.

So I was happy in that winter of 1917, after my transfer to that
town from a remote, snowswept country practice.

2

One month flew by, then another, and a third. 1917 receded and
February 1918 began. I got used to my new life and gradually
began to forget my far-off practice. The hissing, green-shaded
kerosene lamp, the loneliness and the snowdrifts became just a
blurred memory. Ungrateful as I am, I forgot about my front-line
post, where alone and without the least support I had relied on
my own resources to fight disease and extricate myself from the
most hair-raising situations, like a Fenimore Cooper hero.

Now and again, I must admit, when I went to bed with the
pleasant thought that I would shortly fall asleep, fragments of
recollection would pass through my fading consciousness. A
green flash, a flickering lantern, the creak of sleigh-runners . . .
a moan and then darkness, the muffled howl of a snowstorm . . .
then the memory would turn head over heels and vanish into
oblivion.

'I wonder who's in that job now? A young man like me, I
suppose. Ah well, I did my stint, Muryovo and then Gorelovo
hospital . . . February, March, April and, let's say, May as well –
and I will have finished my probationary period. So I shall leave
this splendid town at the end of May and return to Moscow. And

if the revolution calls me to its service, I may yet have some more travelling to do . . . but at all events I shall never see my country practice again . . . Never again . . . Moscow . . . a clinic . . . asphalt, the bright lights . . .'

Such were my thoughts.

'Still, it's a good thing that I spent some time out there in the wilds. It taught me to be brave and nothing frightens me now . . . Is there anything I haven't treated – literally anything? I didn't have any psychiatric cases . . . or did I? No, that's right . . . there was the farm manager who was drinking himself to death. I made rather a mess of treating him, though . . . delirium . . . Surely that's a mental illness? I really ought to read up some psychiatry . . . still, what the hell . . . maybe later, in Moscow. Right now children's diseases are my main concern, and especially the wearisome business of prescribing for children. Hell, if a child's ten years old, for instance, how big a dose of amino-pyrine can I give him? Is it 0.1 or 0.15 grammes? I've forgotten. And if he's three? There are quite enough hideous, unforeseen problems in paediatrics alone, so it's goodbye to my old general practice. But why does that place keep creeping back into my mind so insistently this evening? The green lamp . . . After all, I'm finished with it for the rest of my days . . . well, that's enough of that . . . time for sleep.'

'Letter for you. Someone who happened to come into town brought it.'

'Let's have it.'

The nurse was standing in my hallway. An overcoat with a moth-eaten collar was thrown over her white overall with its hospital badge. Snow was melting on the cheap blue envelope.

'Are you on duty in Casualty Reception?' I asked, yawning.

'Yes, I am.'

'Anyone there?'

'No, it's empty.'

'If any cashesh come in . . .' (I was yawning so hard my pro-nunciation was sloppy) 'come and let me know. I'm going to sleep . . .'

'Yes, doctor. Can I go now?'

'Yes, yes. Off you go.'

She went out. The door squeaked, and I shuffled into the

bedroom in my slippers, clumsily tearing open the envelope as I went. It contained a crumpled oblong prescription form stamped with the address of my old country practice . . . that unforgettable letterhead.

I smiled.

'That's interesting . . . I've been thinking about the place all evening and now this turns up . . . must have had a premonition . . .'

Beneath the letterhead a prescription was written in indelible pencil. Some of the Latin words were illegible, others crossed out.

'What's this? Some prescription gone astray?' I muttered, then stared at the word 'morphini'. 'Well, what's so unusual about this prescription? Ah, yes . . . a four-per-cent solution! Who's been prescribing a four-per-cent solution of morphine? And what for?'

I turned the sheet over. On the reverse side was a letter, written in small spidery handwriting:

11th February 1918.

Dear Colleague,

Forgive me for writing on this old scrap. There's no proper paper at hand. I have fallen seriously ill with something unpleasant. There's no one to help me, and in any case I don't want to ask help of anyone except you.

This is my second month in your old practice, and I know that you are in town and not too far away from me.

On the strength of our friendship at university, I implore you to come and see me as soon as you can – if only for a day, or even an hour. And if you tell me I'm a hopeless case, then I'll believe you. Or perhaps I can still be saved? Perhaps there's still a ray of hope? I beg you to tell no one about the contents of this letter.

Ever yours,

Sergei Polyakov.

'Maria! Go down to casualty at once and fetch me the nurse on duty. What's her name? I forget . . . I mean the one who gave me this letter just now. Hurry.'

'Very good, doctor.'

A few minutes later the nurse was standing in front of me, wet snow on the moulting cat fur that had been used for the collar of her coat.

'Who brought this letter?'

'I don't know who he was. A man with a beard. Said he worked for the co-op and was in town on business.'

'Hmm . . . all right, you can go now. No, wait. I'll just write a note to the Medical Superintendent. Would you take it to him, please, and bring his answer back?'

'All right.'

This is what I wrote to the Medical Superintendent:

13th February 1918.

Dear Pavel Illarionovich,

I have just received a letter from my university friend, Doctor Polyakov. He is working in my previous country practice at Gorelovo, where he is completely alone. He appears to be seriously ill. I think it is my duty to go and see him. With your permission I should like to hand over the dept. to Doctor Rodovich for the day tomorrow and drive out to Polyakov. He has no one else to turn to.

Yours,

Dr Bomgard.

The Medical Superintendent replied:

Dear Vladimir Mikhailovich,
Go.

Petrov.

I spent that evening poring over the railway timetable. The way to reach Gorelovo was as follows: to catch the Moscow mail train at 2 p.m. the following afternoon, travel twenty miles by rail, get off at N. station, and then cover the remaining sixteen miles to Gorelovo hospital by sleigh.

'With luck I should be in Gorelovo tomorrow night,' I reflected as I lay in bed. 'What's the matter with him, I wonder? Typhus? Pneumonia? Neither, I should think . . . because if so, he would simply have written: "I have caught pneumonia". His letter was too vague, even faintly evasive. "Seriously ill . . . something unpleasant . . ."

'What could that mean? Syphilis? Yes, no doubt about it, syphilis. He's appalled, he's concealing it, and he's afraid. But who, I'd like to know, am I going to find to drive me to Gorelovo? It would be just my luck to get to the station at nightfall and find there's no one to take me. No, no, I'll find a way. I'll find someone at the station who has some horses. Should I send him a telegram asking to be met at the station? No use. The telegram won't reach him until the day after I get there. It can't fly to Gorelovo. It would sit at the station until someone was driving out that way. I know that place. What a godforsaken hole!'

The letter on the prescription form lay on my bedside table in the circle of light shed by the lamp, beside it an ashtray bristling with cigarette ends, the outward sign of nagging insomnia. As I tossed about on the crumpled sheet, irritation began to get the better of me, and I started to resent the letter.

After all, if it was nothing worse than, say, syphilis, why didn't he come here himself? Why must I dash through a blizzard to go and see him? Was I supposed to cure him of syphilis or cancer of the aesophagus in one evening? Anyway how could he have cancer? He was two years younger than myself. He was 24 . . . 'Seriously ill'. Sarcoma? It was an absurd, hysterical letter, enough to give the recipient migraine. There, it was starting: the nerve on my temple was starting to twitch; I would wake up in the morning to find that the tension in that nerve had moved to the crown of my head, half my head would feel as if it were clamped in a vice, and I would have to take pyramidon and caffeine. And where would I find pyramidon on a sleigh journey? I should have to borrow one of the hospital's travelling fur coats; I would freeze to death in my own overcoat. What can be the matter with him? '. . . still a ray of hope', indeed! People write that sort of thing in novels, not in sober doctors' letters! Must get to sleep . . . stop thinking about it. It will all be clear tomorrow . . . tomorrow.

I turned the switch and darkness instantly engulfed my room. Sleep . . . that nerve was twitching. But I had no right to be angry with the man for his stupid letter without knowing what the matter was. The man was suffering and he had written to someone else in the way he thought best. And it was unkind to slander him, even mentally, simply because one was worried or suffering from migraine. Perhaps his letter wasn't dishonest or over-dramatic at all. I had not seen Sergei Polyakov for two years, but I remembered him perfectly. He was always a very reasonable man. Yes, obviously some disaster had befallen him . . . And that nerve of mine was giving less trouble. Clearly I would be asleep soon. What was the mechanism of sleep? I had read about it once during my physiology course, but I had found it obscure. I didn't really know what sleep was. How did the brain cells fall asleep?

To be honest, I had no idea. And I was almost certain that the man who wrote that textbook wasn't really very sure either. One theory is as good as another. There was Sergei Polyakov standing in his green medical student's uniform tunic with brass buttons, bending over a zinc-topped table, and there was a corpse on the table.

Hmm, I must be dreaming . . .

3

Tap, tap . . . bang, bang, bang . . . Aha . . . Who's that? What is it? . . . Someone's knocking – hell . . . Where am I? What's going on? Ah, yes, I'm lying in my bed . . . Why are they waking me up? They're allowed to because I'm on call tonight. Wake up, Doctor Bomgard. Maria has just shuffled across the lobby to open the door. What's the time? Half past midnight. That means I've only been asleep for an hour. How's the migraine? Yes, it's there all right.

A gentle knock at the door.

'What is it?'

I slightly opened the door into the dining-room. A nurse's face was looking at me from the dark and I could see at once that it was pale, her eyes wide open with anxiety.

'Who's been brought in?'

'The doctor from the Gorelovo clinic,' the nurse replied in a loud, hoarse voice. 'He's shot himself.'

'*Polyakov?* Impossible! Polyakov?'

'I don't know his name.'

'I see . . . all right, I'll come at once. Run to the Medical Superintendent and wake him up this minute. Tell him I want him urgently in Casualty.'

The nurse rushed off, disappearing in a flash of white.

Two minutes later on the porch a wicked blizzard, dry and stinging, was lashing at my cheeks, lifting the skirts of my coat and freezing my startled body. An unsteady white light was flickering in Casualty Reception. In a swirl of snow on the porch I bumped into the Medical Superintendent, who was hastening in the same direction.

'Is this your friend Polyakov?' he asked, coughing.

'Apparently so. I don't understand it,' I replied as we both hurried inside.

A woman, warmly wrapped up, rose from a bench to meet us. Her eyes, familiar but now tear-stained, gazed at me from under the edge of a red-brown shawl. I recognised her as Marya Vlasievna, a midwife from Gorelovo and my devoted assistant in the labour ward of the Gorelovo hospital.

'Is it Polyakov?' I asked.

'Yes,' Marya Vlasievna answered. 'It was so awful, doctor. I was shaking with terror all the way in case I might not get here in time.'

'When . . . ?'

'This morning at dawn,' Marya Vlasievna muttered. 'The night watchman came running and said he'd heard a shot from the doctor's quarters.'

Under the flickering, inadequate light of the lamp lay Doctor Polyakov. As soon as I caught sight of the stone-like rigidity of his feet I instinctively winced.

They took off his hat, to reveal his hair sticking damply to his scalp. The nurse, Marya Vlasievna, and I set to work on Polyakov and a white gauze bandage, with its spreading yellow and red stains, was revealed beneath his overcoat. His chest rose and fell feebly. I felt his pulse and shivered: the pulse was fading beneath my touch, slowing to a mere flicker and breaking off, then reviving in a cluster of fast, unsteady beats. The surgeon's hand had already reached for his shoulder and was pinching up a fold of pale skin to make a camphor injection. At that moment the wounded man unglued his mouth, revealing a pinkish trickle of blood on it, and with a faint movement of his bluish lips he said in a dry, weak voice:

'To hell with camphor. Forget it.'

'Shut up,' the surgeon retorted, injecting the yellow oil beneath the skin.

'The pericardium seems to be damaged,' Marya Vlasievna whispered, clutching the edge of the table and staring at the wounded man's smooth eyelids (his eyes were shut). Greyish-violet shadows, like the shadows cast at sunset, showed more and more clearly in the hollows around his nostrils, and a fine sweat, like droplets of mercury, was forming in the shadows.

'Revolver?' the surgeon asked, his cheek twitching.

'Automatic.' Marya Vlasievna mouthed the word.

'Hell . . .' the surgeon barked as if in angry frustration, made a brusque gesture and strode away.

I turned to him in alarm, not understanding. Another man's eyes appeared for a moment behind the patient's shoulder – a second doctor had come.

Suddenly Polyakov's mouth twisted into a feeble grimace, like a sleepy person trying to blow a fly off his nose, and then his lower jaw began to move as though he was choking on a lump of food and was trying to swallow it. Anyone who has seen fatal gunshot wounds will be familiar with this movement. Marya Vlasievna frowned painfully and sighed.

'I want . . . Doctor Bomgard,' Polyakov said, almost inaudibly.

'I'm here,' I whispered softly, close to his lips.

'The notebook's for you . . .' Polyakov muttered hoarsely and even more faintly.

With this he opened his eyes and raised them to the gloomy, shadowy ceiling. His dark pupils were lit by an inner light, the whites of his eyes seemed to grow translucent, bluish. His eyes turned upwards, then a film came over them and their momentary brightness faded.

Doctor Polyakov was dead.

4

Night. Nearly dawn. The lamp is burning very brightly because the town is asleep and there is only a light load on the electricity supply. Everything is silent. Polyakov's body is lying in the chapel. Night.

My eyes are reddened from reading, and on the table in front of me lie an open envelope and a sheet of paper. The letter reads:

My dear friend,

I shall not wait for you. I have decided against treatment. It's hopeless. And I don't want to torment myself any longer. I have tried it long enough. I warn others to beware of the white crystals dissolved in 25 parts water. I relied on them too much and they have destroyed me. I bequeath you my diary. You have always struck me as a person of an enquiring nature and a connoisseur of human documents. If you are interested, read the story of my illness.

Farewell.

Ever yours, Sergei Polyakov.

There was a postscript in block capitals:

NO ONE IS TO BE BLAMED FOR MY DEATH.

Doctor S. Polyakov.
13th February, 1918.

Alongside the suicide note was an ordinary school exercise book in a black oilcloth cover. The first half of the pages had been torn out. In the remaining half was a series of jottings; at first they were in ink or pencil in small neat handwriting, then towards the end of the notebook they changed to indelible pencil or red crayon in an untidy, jerky hand and with many of the words abbreviated.

20th January 1917
... and a good thing too. The more remote the better, thank God. I don't want to see people and here I shall see no one, apart from sick peasants, and I don't suppose they are likely to open up my wound. The others, incidentally, have been assigned to practices quite as remote as mine. Our graduating year, not being liable for active service (second-line reservists of the 1916 class), has been posted to local government clinics all over the country. But who cares, anyway? Of my friends, I have only had news of Ivanov and Bomgard. Ivanov chose to go to Archangel Province (de gustibus . . .) and Bomgard, so my woman *feldsher* tells me, is in some godforsaken spot three districts away from here, at Gorelovo. I thought of writing to him, but changed my mind. I don't want to have anything to do with people.

21st January
Blizzard. Nothing else.

25th January
Brilliant sunset. Slight attack of migraine – mixture of amino-pyrine, caffeine and citric acid, 1.0 gramme in powder form. Is it all right to take one gramme? Of course it is.

3rd February

Today I received last week's newspapers. I didn't read them, but couldn't help looking at the theatre page all the same. *Aida* was on last week. That means she was walking on stage and singing: 'Oh, my beloved, come to me . . .'

She has an extraordinary voice. How strange it is that such a clear powerful voice should belong to a woman with such a mean little soul . . .

(*here there is a gap, where two or three pages have been torn out*)

. . . of course, you're being unreasonable, Doctor Polyakov. And what schoolboyish idiocy to use so much filthy language on a woman because she left you! She didn't want to go on living with you, so she went. That's all. Very simple, really. An opera singer fell for a young doctor, lived with him for a year and then walked out.

Did I really want to kill her? *Kill* her? How stupid and pointless. Hopeless. I don't want to think about it any more.

11th February

Perpetual blizzards . . . I'm sick of it. Alone every evening. I light the lamp and sit down. Of course I see people in the daytime, but I do my work mechanically. I've got used to the job, though. It's not as bad as I thought it would be. And having worked in a military hospital has proved to be very useful, because it meant that I wasn't totally incompetent when I came to this place.

Today for the first time I performed the operation of turning a baby in the womb.

There are three of us here, buried under the snow: Anna Kirillovna, *feldsher* and midwife; the male *feldsher*, who is married; and myself. They live in an annexe. And I am on my own.

15th February

Last night an interesting thing happened. I was just going to bed when I suddenly felt pain in the region of my stomach. And what pain! I came out in a cold sweat. I must say that medicine as we know it is a most dubious science. Why, when someone has absolutely nothing wrong with his stomach or gut (such as appendicitis), when his liver and kidneys are in perfect shape, and his bowels are functioning perfectly normally, why should he be stricken one night with such pain that he starts to writhe all over the bed?

Groaning, I reached the kitchen, where the cook and her husband Vlas sleep. I sent Vlas for Anna Kirillovna. She came to my room and had to give me a morphine injection. She said I had turned quite green. From what?

I don't like our *feldsher*. He's unsociable, but Anna Kirillovna is very kind and intelligent. I am amazed that a woman like her, who is still young, can live completely alone in this snowbound tomb. Her husband is a prisoner of war in Germany.

I must give due praise to the man who first extracted morphine from poppyheads. He was a true benefactor of mankind. The pain stopped seven minutes after the injection. Interesting: the pain passed over me in ceaseless waves, so that I had to gasp for breath, as though a red-hot crowbar were being thrust into my stomach and rotated. Four minutes after the injection I was able to distinguish the wave-like nature of the pain.

It would be a good thing if a doctor were able to test many more drugs on himself. He would then have a completely different understanding of their effect. After the injection I slept soundly and well for the first time in months – and I forgot completely about the woman who deceived me.

16th February

During surgery today Anna Kirillovna enquired how I felt and said that this was the first time she had seen me without a frown on my face.

'Do I frown?'

'Very much,' she replied firmly, adding that she had been struck by how taciturn I always was.

'I'm that sort of person.'

But that was a lie. I had always been very cheerful before my disastrous love affair.

Dusk has set in early. I am alone in my quarters. The pain came again this evening, but it was not acute – a mere shadow of yesterday's pain. I felt it somewhere behind my breast bone. Fearing a recurrence of yesterday's attack, I injected myself in the thigh with one centigramme. The pain ceased almost instant-aneously. A good thing Anna Kirillovna left the phial behind.

18th
Four injections. No harm in that.

21st February
Anna Kirillovna is behaving very oddly – just as though I weren't a doctor at all! $1\frac{1}{2}$ syringes $=0.015$ grammes morph.? Yes.

1st March
Take care, Doctor Polyakov!
Nonsense.

Twilight.
It is two weeks now since I last thought about the woman who deceived me. I no longer have the tune of her aria as Amneris on the brain. I am very proud of that. I am a man.
Anna Kirillovna has become my mistress. It was inevitable. We are imprisoned on a desert island.

A change has come over the snow; it seems to have turned greyer. There are no more savage frosts, but snowstorms still blow up from time to time.

For the first minute there is a sensation of being touched on my neck. The touch grows warmer and spreads. In the second minute there is a sudden surge of cold in the pit of my stomach, after which I start to think with unusual clarity and experience a burst of mental energy. All unpleasant sensations stop completely. Man's inner powers are manifested at their absolute peak. And if I had not been spoiled by my medical training, I would say that a man can only work normally after an injection of morphine. After all, what good is a man when the slightest attack of neuralgia can knock him completely off balance?

Anna K. is frightened. Calmed her, saying that since childhood I have been remarkable for having tremendous willpower.

2nd March
Rumours of great events. It seems that Nicholas II has been deposed.

I shall go to bed very early – about nine o'clock.

And my sleep will be sweet.

10th March
A revolution is going on 'up there'.

The days are getting longer, the twilight seems faintly tinged with blue.

Never before have I had such dreams at dawn. They are double dreams. The main one, I would say, is made of glass. It is transparent.

This is what happens: I see a lighted lamp, fearfully bright, from which blazes a stream of many-coloured light. Amneris, swaying like a green feather, is singing. An unearthly orchestra is playing with a full, rich sound – although I cannot really convey this in words. In short, in a normal dream music is soundless (in a normal dream? What dream, may one ask, is ever normal! But I'm joking) . . . soundless, but in my dream the music sounds quite heavenly. And best of all I can make the music louder or softer at will. It reminds me of a passage in *War and Peace* in which Petya Rostov experiences the same phenomenon when half asleep. Leo Tolstoy is a remarkable writer!

As to the dream's transparency, what happens is that through the iridescent colours of *Aida* the edge of my desk shows through with complete reality, through the study door I can see the lamp, the gleaming floor, and behind the wave of sound from the Bolshoi Theatre orchestra I can clearly hear the welcome tread of footsteps like muffled castanets.

That means it is eight o'clock, Anna K. is coming to tell me what is happening in the surgery.

She doesn't realise that I don't need waking, that I can hear everything and can talk to her.

I tried the following experiment yesterday:

Anna: Sergei Vasilievich . . .
Myself: I'm listening . . . (to the music, sotto voce: 'Louder!')
   The music: a powerful chord of D sharp.
Anna: Twenty patients on the register.

Amneris sings . . .

But it can't be conveyed on paper.

Is there any harm in these dreams? Not at all. When they are over I get up, feel wide awake and cheerful. I've even started to take an interest in the work, which I never did before – not surprisingly, since I could never think of anything but my former mistress.

Whereas now I don't worry any more.

19th March

Last night I had a quarrel with Anna K.

'I'm not going to make up the solution any more.'

I started to try and persuade her.

'Don't be silly, my dear. I'm not a little boy, am I?'

'I won't do it. It'll kill you.'

'All right, please yourself. Don't you realise, though, that I've got pains in my chest?'

'Get it treated.'

'Where?'

'Take a holiday. Morphine's not a cure.' Then after a moment's thought she added: 'I can never forgive myself for having made up a second phial for you.'

'What do you think I am – an addict?'

'Yes, you're becoming an addict.'

'So you won't?'

'No, I won't.'

It was then that I first discovered in myself a nasty tendency to lose my temper and, worse, to shout at people when I am in the wrong.

However, this did not happen at once. I went into my bedroom and had a look: there was a very little left in the bottom of the phial. I drew it into the syringe, and it only filled a quarter of it. I threw the syringe away, almost breaking it, and shuddered. Carefully, I picked it up and examined it – not a single crack. I sat in the bedroom for twenty minutes. When I came out, she was gone.

Imagine – I couldn't bear it and went to look for her. I knocked on the lighted window of her quarters. Wrapped in a scarf, she came out on to the porch. The night was silent, the snow powdery and dry. Far away in the sky was a hint of coming spring.

'Please, Anna Kirillovna, give me the keys to the dispensary.'

She whispered: 'No, I won't.'

'Kindly give me the keys to the dispensary. I'm speaking as a doctor.'

In the twilight I saw her expression change. She turned very white, her eyes seemed to sink into her head and they darkened. She replied in a voice which stirred me to pity. But at once my anger surged up again.

She said: 'Why, why must you talk like this? Oh Sergei Vasilievich – I pity you.'

Just then she drew her hands from under her shawl and I saw that she was holding the keys. She had obviously gone over to my consulting room and removed them.

'Give me the keys!' I said roughly.

And I snatched them out of her hand.

I set off towards the white-painted hospital building, picking my way along the rotten, swaying duckboards. Rage was boiling inside me, chiefly because I had not the slightest idea how to make up a morphine solution for hypodermic injection. I'm a doctor, not an assistant! I trembled as I went.

I could hear her walking behind me like a faithful dog. Tenderness welled up inside me, but I suppressed it. I turned round, bared my teeth and said:

'Are you going to do it or not?'

She gave a despairing gesture as much as to say 'What does it matter?' and answered quietly:

'All right, I'll do it.'

An hour later I was myself again, and I naturally asked her to forgive me for my absurd rudeness. I don't know what happened to me: I was always polite before.

Then she did something extraordinary. She fell to her knees, clasped my hands and said:

'I'm not angry with you. I know now that you're lost. I know it now. And I curse myself for giving you that first injection.'

I calmed her down as best I could, assuring her that none of this was her doing, that I was responsible for my own behaviour. I promised her that the very next day I would make a serious start on breaking the habit and would reduce the dosage.

'How much did you inject just now?'

'Not much. Three syringes of a 1% solution.'

She clasped her head and said nothing.

'There's no cause for you to worry.'

In my heart of hearts I understood her concern. The fact is that hydrochloric morphium is terrifying stuff. You can very quickly get used to it. But surely mild habituation is not the same as becoming an addict?

To tell the truth, this woman is the only person I can really trust. She ought really to be my wife. I've forgotten the other woman, quite forgotten her. However, I have morphine to thank for that.

8th April 1917
This is torture.

9th April
This horrible spring weather.

The devil is in this phial. Cocaine – the devil in a phial!

This is its effect: on injecting one syringe of a 2% solution, you feel almost immediately a state of calm, which quickly grows into a delightful euphoria. This lasts for only a minute or two, then it vanishes without a trace as though it had never been. Then comes pain, horror, darkness.

Outside, the spring thaw is in noisy spate, blackbirds fly from branch to bare branch and in the distance the forest pierces the sky like a jagged row of black bristles; behind the trees, colouring a quarter of the sky, glows the first spring sunset.

I pace diagonally across the big, empty, lonely room in my quarters, from the door to the window and back again. How many times can I cover that stretch of floor? Fifteen or sixteen times, not more; then I have to turn round and go into the bedroom. Lying on a piece of gauze beside a phial is the syringe. I pick it up and after giving my puncture-riddled thigh a careless smear of iodine, I dig the needle into the skin. Far from feeling any pain, I have a foretaste of the euphoria which will overtake me in a moment. And here it comes. I am aware of its onset, for as Vlas the night watchman sits in the porch playing the accordion, the faint, muffled snatches of music sound like angelic voices, and the harsh bass chords wheezing from the bellows ring out like a celestial choir. But now comes the moment when, by some mysterious law that is not to be found in any book on pharmacology, the cocaine inside me turns into something different. I know what it is: it is a mixture of my blood and the devil himself. The sound of Vlas' accordion music falters and I hate the man, while the sunset growls restlessly and burns my entrails. This feeling comes over me several times in the course of the evening, until I realise that I have poisoned myself. My heart begins to beat so hard that I can feel it thumping when I put my hands to my temples . . . Then my whole being sinks into the abyss and there are moments when I wonder whether Doctor Polyakov will ever come back to life.

13th April
I, the unfortunate Doctor Polyakov, who became addicted to morphine in February of this year, warn anyone who may suffer the same fate not to attempt to replace morphine with cocaine. Cocaine is a most foul and insidious poison. Yesterday Anna barely managed to revive me with camphor injections and today I am half dead.

6th May 1917
It is a long time since I last wrote anything in my diary. A pity, because in fact this is not a diary but a pathological history. Not only do I have a natural professional interest in it, but it is my only friend in the world (if one doesn't count my sad and often tearful mistress Anna). So if I am to record the progress of my disease, here it is: I inject myself with morphine twice every twenty-four hours – at five o'clock in the afternoon (after supper) and at midnight before going to bed. Two syringes of a 3% solution; my dose is thus 50 milligrammes. A fair amount!

My previous notes must sound somewhat hysterical. In fact there is nothing particularly unusual or alarming about my condition. It does not in the least affect my capacity to work. On the contrary, I live through the day on the previous night's injection.

I cope splendidly with operations, I am irreproachably careful when prescribing, and I give my professional oath that my addiction causes no harm to my patients. I pray that it never will. But something else does worry me: I keep thinking that other people may find out about my vice. During consultation hours I am disturbed by the thought of my assistant's grim, searching look behind my back.

Nonsense! He'll never guess. There's nothing to give me away. The pupils of my eyes can only betray me in the evening, and I never see him in the evening.

To make up for the terrible drain on the stock of morphine in our dispensary, I drove into the local town. There, too, I went through a nasty few minutes. I had taken care to fill out my order with all kinds of stuff such as caffeine (of which we had plenty), but as the storekeeper took it he said dubiously:

'Forty grammes of morphine?'

I did not know where to look, and felt myself blushing like a guilty schoolboy. He said:

'We haven't got that much. I can give you ten grammes.'

He really did not have that quantity, but I had the impression that he had discovered my secret; his probing eyes were boring into me and this made me nervous and jumpy.

My pupils, I have decided, are the only danger signs, and for that reason I shall make it a rule not to see anyone in the evening. For this, incidentally, there could be no more convenient place than my isolated practice; it is six months since I have seen anyone except my patients, and they have not the slightest interest in me.

18th May

A sultry night. A thunderstorm is brewing, black storm clouds building up beyond the forest. A moment ago there came a pale warning flash of lightning. The storm has begun.

A book is open in front of me and this is what it has to say about the symptoms of morphine withdrawal:

'. . . morbid anxiety, a nervous depressed condition, irritability, weakening of the memory, occasional hallucinations and a mild impairment of consciousness . . .'

I have not experienced any hallucinations, but I can only say that the rest of this description is dull, pedestrian and totally inadequate. 'Depressed condition' indeed! Having suffered from this appalling malady, I hereby enjoin all doctors to be more compassionate toward their patients. What overtakes the addict deprived of morphine for a mere hour or two is not a 'depressed condition': it is slow death. Air is insubstantial, gulping it down is useless . . . there is not a cell in one's body that does not crave . . . but crave what? This is something which defies analysis and explanation. In short, the individual ceases to exist: he is eliminated. The body which moves, agonises and suffers is a corpse. It wants nothing, can think of nothing but morphine. To die of thirst is a heavenly, blissful death compared with the craving for morphine. The feeling must be something like that of a man buried alive, clawing at the skin on his chest in the effort to catch the last tiny bubbles of air in his coffin, or of a heretic at the stake, groaning and writhing as the first tongues of flame lick at his feet.

Death. A dry, slow death. That is what lurks behind that clinical, academic phrase 'a depressed condition'.

I can't hold out. I have just had to inject myself. A deep breath. And another.

Feeling better. Ah . . . there it is . . . a stab of cold in the pit of my stomach, a taste of peppermint . . .

Three syringes of a 3% solution. That will last me until midnight.

Nonsense. That last entry was nonsense. It's not as bad as that. Sooner or later I'll give it up . . . but now I need sleep, sleep.

This idiotic, agonising battle against morphine is wearing me out.

(*The next couple of dozen or so pages are torn out.*)

. . . ing.
. . . gain vomited at 4.30 a.m.
When I feel better I shall record this appalling experience.

14th November 1917
So having run away from Doctor . . .'s (*the name has been carefully crossed out*) clinic in Moscow, I am home again. The rain is

streaming down and shrouding the outside world from my sight.
Long may it do so. I don't need the world any more, and no one
in the world needs me. I was in the clinic while the shooting and
the coup d'état took place, but the idea of abandoning the cure
had begun insidiously to grow in my mind even before the fighting
started in the streets of Moscow. I have the morphine to thank
for making me brave. I'm not afraid of rifle fire now. After all,
what can possibly frighten a man obsessed by one thing only –
the divine, wonder-working crystals? The nurse, utterly terrified
by the crash of gunfire . . .

(*page torn out*)

. . . pped out that page so that no one should read the disgraceful
account of how a professional man ran away like a cowardly thief
and stole his own suit.

And not only my suit; I was so desperate that I also took a
hospital shirt. Next day, having given myself an injection, I
pulled myself together and returned to Doctor N. His attitude
was one of pity, but even so I sensed contempt behind his pity,
which was wrong of him: he is after all a psychiatrist and ought
to realise that I am not always in control of myself. I am a
sick man. He should not despise me. I gave back the hospital
shirt.

'Thank you,' he said. 'And what do you propose to do now?'

Being then in a state of euphoria, I said cheerfully: 'I have
decided to go back to my practice; my leave is over, anyway. I am
very grateful to you for your help and I feel decidedly better. I
shall continue the treatment at home.'

To this he replied: 'You are not in the least better. I find it
ludicrous that you should say this to me. One look at your pupils
is enough. Who do you think you're talking to?'

'I can't throw off the addiction all at once, professor . . .
especially now, with all that's going on around us . . . the gunfire
has made me a nervous wreck.'

'It's over now. We have a new government. Go back to bed.'

As he said this I remembered it all: the chilly corridors, the
blank, shiny oil-painted walls . . . and myself limping past them
like a lame dog, waiting for something . . . For what? For a hot
bath? No, for a wretchedly small injection of 5 milligrammes of
morphine. I can stay alive on a dose of that size, but only just.
And the anguish remains, weighing me down like lead, just as it

did before. Sleepless nights, the shirt which I tore to shreds as I begged them to let me go.

No. They have invented morphine, extracting it from the dried, rattling seed-heads of that divine plant, so let them damn well find a painless cure for it! I shook my head obstinately. At that the professor stood up and I suddenly rushed for the door in terror. I thought he meant to lock me in and keep me in the clinic by force.

The professor turned red in the face. 'I am not a warder,' he said with some irritation, 'and this isn't the Butyrki Prison. Sit down and relax. Two weeks ago you claimed you were completely normal. Yet now . . .' Expressively, he imitated my gesture of fear. 'I'm not keeping you here.'

'Professor, give me back my committal certificate. I beg you.' my voice quavered pitifully.

'By all means.'

With a jingle of keys he opened a drawer in his desk and handed me the certificate, on which I had voluntarily committed myself to taking the full two-month cure and had agreed that they should restrain me from leaving the clinic – the usual wording.

As I took the certificate with a trembling hand and stuffed it into my pocket I mumbled:

'Thank you.'

Then I got up to go and started to leave.

'Doctor Polyakov!' His voice rang out behind me. I turned round, my hand on the doorknob. 'Listen,' he said, 'think it over. You must realise that you will inevitably land up in a psychiatric hospital at a slightly, er . . . later stage. And when you do, you will be in a far worse condition. So far I have at least been able to deal with you as a doctor. But later you will be in a state of total mental collapse. Strictly speaking, my dear fellow, you are not fit to practise and I shall be breaking the law if I do not notify your local medical authority to that effect.'

I shuddered and plainly felt the colour drain from my face (although I was pale enough already).

'I beg you, professor,' I said dully, 'not to tell them anything . . . I'd be struck off with ignominy for being an addict . . . Surely you wouldn't do that to me?'

'Oh, very well then, go,' he shouted irritably. 'I won't say anything. All the same, you'll be back.'

I went, and I swear that I was racked with pain and shame all the way home. Why?

The answer's simple. Ah, my diary, my faithful friend – you at least won't give me away, will you? It was not because of the suit, but because I also stole some morphine from the hospital. Three cubes in crystal form and ten grammes of 1% solution.

But this in itself is not the only thing which interests me. The key was in the lock of the hospital's drug cabinet. Supposing it had not been. Would I have smashed open the cupboard? Would I? In all honesty?

Yes, I would.

So Doctor Polyakov is a thief. I must remember to tear that page out.

Still, he was exaggerating when he said I was unfit to practise. It is absolutely true that I am degenerating; the break-up of my moral personality has set in. But I can still work, and I am incapable of inflicting harm or wrong on a single one of my patients.

Why did I steal? It's very simple. During the fighting and unrest connected with the coup d'état, I thought I might not be able to get any more supplies of morphine. But when the disturbances died down, I managed to find some in a suburban pharmacy – 15 grammes of 1% solution, which to me was almost worse than useless, as one dose would have required nine injections. What was more, I had to put up with being humiliated: the pharmacist demanded a rubber stamp on my prescription and glowered at me suspiciously. Next day, however, all was well again when I was given 20 grammes in crystal form without the slightest delay, having written out a prescription for the hospital (adding, of course, an order for caffeine and aspirin as well). But why, after all, should I have to hide and feel afraid? I'm behaving as if the words 'drug addict' were branded on my forehead. Whose business is it besides mine, for heaven's sake?

In any case, have I really gone so far downhill? I cite this diary as evidence. The entries are fragmentary, but then I'm not a writer by profession. Do they sound unbalanced? I would say that my reasoning is entirely sane.

For an addict there is one pleasure of which no one can deprive him – his ability to spend his time in absolute solitude. And solitude means deep, significant thought; it means, calm, contemplation – and wisdom.

The night flows on, black and silent. Somewhere out there is the bare leafless forest, beyond it the river, the chill air of autumn. Far away lies the strife-torn, restless city of Moscow. Nothing concerns me, I need nothing and there is nowhere for me to go.

The flame in my lamp burns softly; I want to rest after my adventures in Moscow and forget them.

And I have forgotten them.

18th November
Frost. The ground dry and hard. I went out for a walk along the path by the river, because I hardly ever get any fresh air.

I may be in a state of moral decay, but I am nevertheless making an effort to arrest it. This morning, for instance, I did not have an injection (I am now injecting myself with three syringes of 4% solution three times daily). Awkward. I feel sorry for Anna. Each extra per cent causes her agony, which saddens me. She is such a wonderful person.

So when the pains began I decided to suffer awhile (how Professor N. would approve if only he could see me!) by delaying my injection, and set off for a walk by the river.

It was completely deserted. Not a sound, not so much as a rustle. Dusk had not yet fallen, but it was in the air, lurking in the marshland, creeping between the tussocks and tree-stumps . . . slowly closing in on Levkovo hospital, while I shuffled along leaning on my stick (to tell the truth, I have grown somewhat weaker recently).

Then I noticed a little old woman with yellow hair coming

quickly towards me up the slope from the river, moving so fast that I could not see her feet under her colourful, bell-shaped skirts. At first sight I paid no attention to her and felt no alarm; she was after all just an old peasant woman. Then it struck me as odd that she was bareheaded and wearing only a blouse, because it was so cold. A moment later I began to wonder – where was she from? Who was she? When consulting hours at Levkovo are over, the peasant sleighs all drive away and there is no one to be seen for miles around – nothing but mist, marshland and woods. Suddenly I felt a cold sweat break out up and down my spine and I realised: the old woman was not running but actually flying, without touching the ground. This was bad enough; but what made me scream aloud was the fact that she was holding a pitchfork in both hands. Why was I so frightened? I fell on to one knee, holding out my hands to shield myself from the sight, then I turned and ran, stumbling, for home and safety, praying that my heart would not give out before I could reach my warm room, see my flesh-and-blood Anna . . . and take some morphine . . .

And I came home at a run.

What nonsense. A meaningless, chance hallucination.

19th November
Vomiting. A bad sign.

My conversation with Anna on the night of the 21st:

Anna: The *feldsher* knows.
Myself: Does he? So what? I don't care.
Anna: If you don't leave this place and go into town, I shall kill myself. D'you hear? Look at your hands.
Myself: They're trembling slightly. That doesn't stop me working, though.
Anna: Just look at them – they're absolutely transparent. Nothing but skin and bone. And take a look at your face. Listen, Sergei – go away, I implore you . . .
Myself: What about you?
Anna: Go away, go away. You're dying.
Myself: Don't exaggerate. Still, I must admit I don't understand why I've suddenly weakened so quickly. After all, it's less than a

year since this illness started. I suppose it's due to my constitution.

Anna (sadly): What can bring you back to life? Perhaps your Amneris, that opera singer?

Myself: Oh no, don't worry. I've got over her, thanks to the drug. I have morphine instead of her.

Anna: Oh my God . . . what am I to do?

I thought that women like Anna only existed in novels. If ever I'm cured, I shall stay with her for the rest of my life. I only hope her husband never comes back from Germany.

27th December
I haven't touched my diary for a long time. I am wrapped up for the journey, the horses are waiting. Bomgard has left his practice at Gorelovo and I am being sent to replace him. A woman doctor is coming to take over my practice.

Anna is staying here. She will drive over to see me. Even though it is twenty miles away.

We have firmly decided that I will take a month's sick leave from 1st January and go back to the professor in Moscow. I shall sign a form again and suffer another month of inhuman torture in his clinic.

Farewell, Levkovo. Au revoir, Anna.

1918
January
I didn't go. I can't leave those life-giving crystals.

I would die if I took a cure now. I am becoming more and more convinced that I don't need a cure at all.

15th January
Vomiting in the morning.
Three syringes of 4% solution at dusk.
Three syringes of 4% solution late at night.

16th January
Operation day today, so I have to endure a long period of abstinence – from night time until 6 p.m.

At dusk – always my worst time – I clearly heard a voice in my room, monotonous and threatening, repeating my name and patronymic:

'Sergei Vasilievich. Sergei Vasilievich.'

It stopped as soon as I injected myself.

17th January
Blizzard today, so no consultation. During the hours of abstention I read a textbook of psychiatry and it appalled me. I am done for; there's no hope.

During abstinence I am terrified by the slightest sound and I find people detestable. I am afraid of them. In the euphoric phase I love everyone, although I prefer solitude.

I must be careful at Gorelovo – there is a *feldsher* here and two midwives. I must take the greatest possible care not to give myself away. I shall succeed, because by now I am very experienced. No one will find out, as long as I have a supply of morphine. I either prepare the solution myself or send a prescription to Anna in good time. Once she made a clumsy attempt to substitute a 2% for a 5% solution. She brought it herself from Levkovo in bitter cold and a raging snowstorm.

This caused a violent quarrel between us that night. I persuaded her not to do it again. I have told the staff here that I am ill, after racking my brains for a long time to decide what illness to invent. I said that I had rheumatism in my legs and severe neuralgia. They have been warned that I am going away in February for a month's sick leave to take a cure in Moscow. All is going smoothly. No trouble with my work. I avoid operating on the days when I am overcome by uncontrollable vomiting and retching. Because of this, I've had to add gastric catarrh to my alleged ailments. Too many diseases for one person, I fear.

The staff here are very sympathetic and are themselves urging me to take sick leave.

Outward appearance: thin, pale with a waxen pallor.

I took a bath and afterwards weighed myself on the hospital scales. Last year I weighed 148 lbs (67 kgs); now I weigh 120 lbs (54 kgs). I had a fright as I watched the needle on the dial, but the shock soon passed.

My forearms and thighs are a mass of unhealed abscesses. I don't know how to prepare sterile solutions, besides which I have injected myself with an unsterilised syringe on about three occasions when I was in a great hurry to go out on my rounds.

This can't be allowed to go on.

18th January

I had the following hallucination:

I was sitting in front of a blank, dark window expecting some kind of pale figures to appear. The suspense was intolerable. Yet there was nothing there except the blind. I fetched some gauze from the hospital and draped it over the window. I was unable to think of a rational excuse for my action.

Hell, why *should* I have to find a pretext for every single thing I do? What I am living is not a normal existence, but torture.

Do I express my thoughts lucidly?
I think I do.
What is my life? An absurdity.

19th January

Today during the break in consulting hours, when we were re-laxing and having a smoke in the dispensary, the *feldsher* started to tell a story as he wrapped powders in little screws of paper. Laughing for some reason, he described how a woman *feldsher* had become a morphine addict; unable to get the drug, she had swallowed half a tumbler full of an infusion of opium. I did not not know where to look during this painful story. Why on earth did he find it amusing? Why?

I slunk furtively out of the dispensary.

I wanted to say: 'What's so funny about that affliction?' But I restrained myself.

In my position I cannot afford to be too rude to people.

That *feldsher* is as cruel as those psychiatrists who are so utterly, completely incapable of helping their patients.

Totally incapable.

I wrote the last entry during a period of abstinence and much of what I said was unfair.

A moonlit night. I am lying down, feeling weak after a fit of vomiting. I can hardly lift my hands, so am scribbling my thoughts in pencil. My mind is calm and serene. For a few hours I am happy. Soon I shall sleep. Overhead is the moon, surrounded by a halo. Nothing upsets me after an injection.

1st February
Anna has arrived. She looks sallow and ill.

I have driven her to the end of her tether. This terrible wrong weighs on my conscience.

I have given her my oath that I will leave here in mid-February.

Will I do as I have promised?

Yes, I will.

Provided I am still alive.

3rd February
So now I am poised at the top of a slope. It is icy, slippery and as endlessly long as the hill down which Kaj's sledge ran in Hans Andersen's fairy tale. This is my last ride down this slope, and I know what is waiting for me at the bottom. Oh Anna, terrible grief will soon be your reward for having loved me . . .

11th February
I have decided to appeal to Bomgard. Why to him? Because he is not a psychiatrist; because he's young and we were friends at university. He is healthy and tough yet kind-hearted, if I have gauged his character right. Perhaps he will be reli . . . sympathetic. He will think of some solution. He can take me to Moscow if he wants to. I can't go to him. My sick leave has been approved.

I am not going to work in the hospital, but am lying in bed.

I swore at the *feldsher*. He just laughed . . . It doesn't matter. He had come to report to me, and offered to sound my respiration and heartbeat.

I refused to let him. Must I go on finding excuses for refusing? I am sick of inventing pretexts.

The note has been sent off to Bomgard.

People! Won't anyone help me?

I am lapsing into outbursts of self-pity. If anybody were to read this they would find it maudlin and insincere. But no one will read it.

Before writing to Bomgard, all my memories came back to me. I had a particular recollection of a Moscow railway station in November, when I was running away from the clinic. What an appalling evening that was. I had gone to a lavatory in the station to inject my stolen morphine. It was a nightmare. People were banging on the door, shouting and swearing at me for spending too long in there, my hands were shaking and the doorhandle was rattling so violently that I thought the door would burst open at any moment.

This was when I started to develop abscesses.

I wept the night that I remembered that incident.

12th Night

I wept again. Why does this disgusting weakness come over me at night?

13th February 1918. Dawn, Gorelovo

I can congratulate myself: I have not had an injection for fourteen hours! Fourteen! An unbelievable number. Murky yellowish light of dawn. Soon I shall be quite cured.

On mature reflection I don't need Bomgard, or anyone else for that matter. It would be shameful to prolong my life a minute more. Certainly not a life like mine. The remedy is right beside me. Why didn't I think of it before?

Well, let's get it over with. I owe nothing to anyone. I have destroyed only myself. And Anna. What else can I do?

Time will heal all, as Amneris sang. It's easy and simple enough for her.

This notebook is for Bomgard. That's all . . .

5

I read Sergei Polyakov's notes at dawn on the 14th February 1918 in that faraway little country town. They are reproduced here in full, without the slightest alteration. Not being a psychiatrist, I cannot say with certainty whether or not they are instructive or useful though I believe they are.

Now that ten years have passed, the pity and terror evoked by this diary have, of course, faded. This is natural, but on re-reading the jottings, now, when Polyakov's body has long since decayed and the memory of him vanished for ever, I still find them interesting. Are they of value? I shall not presume to make a firm judgement on that point. Anna K. died of typhus in 1922 in the same country practice where she had always worked. Amneris – Polyakov's first mistress – has gone abroad and will not return.

Should I publish the diary which was entrusted to me?

I should. Here it is.

Doctor Bomgard.

The Murderer

Doctor Yashvin gave a curiously wry, ironic grin and asked: 'May I tear the leaf off the calendar? It's exactly midnight, so now it's the second of the month.'

'Go ahead, by all means,' I answered.

Yashvin took hold of a corner of the topmost leaf with his slender white fingers and carefully tore it off, revealing another cheap, nasty sheet of paper printed with the figure '2' and the word 'Friday'. But something on that greyish page seemed to seize his interest. He narrowed his eyes as he looked at it, then raised his glance and gazed into the distance; he was evidently seeing some mysterious scene visible only to himself, somewhere beyond the wall of my room – or perhaps far beyond the Moscow night and the raw grip of a February frost.

'What's on his mind?' I wondered, glancing at him. I had always been intrigued by Doctor Yashvin. Somehow his appearance did not match his profession. Strangers always took him for an actor. He had dark hair but a very white skin, and this made him both conspicuous and attractive. He was very smoothly shaven, he dressed impeccably, was extremely fond of the theatre and could discuss it with great taste and knowledge. But what really distinguished him from our interns and from my other guests that evening were his shoes. There were five of us in the room and four were wearing cheap box-calf boots with clumsy, rounded toes, but Doctor Yashvin wore pointed patent leather shoes and yellow spats. I must add, though, that Yashvin's dandyish appearance was never exactly offensive and, to give him his due, he was a very good doctor. He was bold, successful, and most important, he found time to keep up his reading, in spite of regular visits to *The Valkyrie* and *The Barber of Seville*.

His shoes, however, were not the most interesting thing about him. What fascinated me was one remarkable characteristic: his gift, which he would occasionally display, of being a marvellous raconteur, even though he was usually a quiet and decidedly withdrawn man. He spoke very deliberately without striving for effect, without the average man's redundant verbiage and humming and hawing, and always on very interesting topics. The reserved, elegant doctor seemed to light up, his pale right hand making occasional short, smooth, economical gestures as if he were punctuating his account with little milestones in the air; he never smiled when telling something funny, and his similes were sometimes so apt and colourful that as I listened to him I was always disturbed by one thought:

'You are a very good doctor, but you've chosen the wrong career. You should have been a writer.'

Now, too, this thought flashed through my head, even though Yashvin was not talking but screwing up his eyes at the figure '2' and at some imaginary object in the distance.

'What is he looking at? Maybe there's a picture.' I looked over my shoulder and saw that the picture was totally uninteresting. It depicted an improbable-looking horse with an exaggerated chest and next to it an engine. The caption read: 'Comparative size of horse (one horsepower) and engine (500 horsepower).'

'This is all nonsense,' I said, continuing the conversation. 'Banal prejudice. People are most unfair to doctors and to us surgeons in particular. Just think: a man does a hundred appendectomies and the hundred and first patient expires on the operating table. Is that murder?'

'They're bound to say it is,' Doctor Gips replied.

'And if the patient is a married woman, the husband will come to the surgery and throw a chair at you,' Doctor Plonsky affirmed confidently; he even smiled, and we all smiled, although there is nothing very funny about people hurling chairs around the surgery.

'I can't bear it, because it rings so false, when someone says penitentially: "I have killed, ah me, I'm a murderer",' I continued. 'No doctor murders anyone, and if someone dies on you, then it's just bad luck. No, really, it's simply a joke! Murder is not part of our profession. How can it be? I call murder the premeditated killing of a person, or if you insist, the desire to kill him. A surgeon with a pistol in his hand – that, I'll admit, might be murder. But I've never met any such surgeon in my life, nor am I likely to.'

As Doctor Yashvin suddenly turned his head towards me, I noticed that his expression had become grim. He said:

'I am at your service.'

At the same time he tugged at his tie and once again gave a crooked grin with one corner of his mouth, though not with his eyes.

We looked at him in astonishment.

'What do you mean?' I asked.

'I have killed a man,' he explained.

'When?' I asked absurdly.

Yashvin pointed to the number '2' and answered:

'It's an extraordinary coincidence. As soon as you started talking about death, I noticed the calendar and saw that it was the second. But in any case I remember this night every year. You see, seven years ago to the very night, and even, indeed . . .' Yashvin pulled out his black watch and glanced at it, '. . . yes, almost to the very hour, on the night of the 1st and 2nd of February, I killed him.'

'A patient?' Gips asked.

'Yes, a patient.'

'But not deliberately?' I asked.

'Oh, I can guess,' Plonsky, the sceptic, remarked through clenched teeth. 'He probably had cancer and was dying in torment, and you gave him ten times the normal dose of morphine.'

'No, morphine had nothing to do with it. Nor did he have any sort of cancer. The weather was frosty – I remember it perfectly – about fifteen degrees below zero, and there were stars in the sky. Ah, what stars there are in the Ukraine. I've been living in Moscow almost seven years, but I still feel drawn to my homeland. My heart aches, I get a terrible urge to board a train and be off. To see the cliffs covered in snow, the Dnieper . . . there's no more beautiful city in the world than Kiev.'

Yashvin put the calendar page in his wallet, curled himself up in the armchair and went on:

'It was a grim city, at a grim time . . . and I saw terrible things, such as you in Moscow never saw. This was in 1919, on the first of February as it happens. It was twilight, about six o'clock in the evening. I found myself doing something rather strange in that twilight. A lamp was burning on the desk in my study, the room was warm and cosy, but I was sitting on the floor bending over a small suitcase, cramming it with all sorts of rubbish, and whispering to myself:

'"Must get away, must get away . . ."

'I would put in a shirt and take it out again – the damn thing wouldn't fit in. The case was tiny, my underpants took up so much space, then there were hundreds of cigarettes and my stethoscope, all of which were bulging out of the bag. I flung the shirt away and pricked up my ears. The windowframes were sealed with putty for the winter, so the sound was deadened, but you could still hear it . . . far, far away there was a low rumble, like something being dragged along – boo-oom, boo-oom . . . Heavy guns. The echo would die away, and then silence. I looked out of the window – I lived on a steep slope, at the top of St Aleksei's Hill, and I could see the whole of Podol, the Lower City. Night was drawing in from the west, the direction of the Dnieper, enveloping the houses, and rows of windows were lighting up. Then followed another salvo. And each time a rumble came from the far side of the Dnieper, I would whisper:

'"Go on, keep it up."

'This was the situation: the whole city knew that Petlyura was just about to abandon it – if not that night, then the next night. The Bolsheviks were advancing from the west bank of the Dnieper and rumour had it that they were in great strength. I must admit that the whole city was not merely impatient but even enthusiastic for their arrival. The atrocities committed by Petlyura's men in Kiev for the last month that they held it were beyond anything you can imagine. Pogroms were whipped up every minute and people were murdered daily, especially Jews of course. Whenever they wanted to requisition something, cars would hurtle through the city manned by troops wearing fur hats with tassels of red braid, and there had been ceaseless gunfire in the distance for the last few days. Night and day. Everyone was in a state of something like exhaustion, with a frightened, hunted look. Only the day before, two corpses had been lying in the snow under my windows for half a day. One was wearing a grey overcoat and the other a black peasant shirt; neither had boots. Passers-by either shied away or gathered in crowds to stare, and a few bareheaded peasant women darted out of gateways, shook their fists at the sky and shouted:

'"Just you wait till the Bolsheviks come."

'The sight of these two wretched men, killed for some unknown reason, was sickening, and so in the end I too started looking forward to the Bolsheviks' arrival. They were coming nearer and nearer. Darkness was falling, and from the distance came rumblings, as if in the very bowels of the earth. So with my lamp giving out a light that was both reassuring and yet disturbing, I was completely alone in the flat; my books were scattered everywhere (for in all this chaos I had cherished the insane hope of studying for a higher degree) and I myself was crouched over a suitcase.

'To tell you the truth, events had seized me by the hair and dragged me along with them: everything had been happening as though in some hellish nightmare. I had come back that evening from a workers' hospital in the suburbs where I was an intern in the female surgery department, and on my arrival I had found an envelope stuck in the letter-box with an unpleasantly official look. I tore it open there and then on the landing, read the contents and sat down on the top stair.

'The note, typed in blue-black ink, was in Ukrainian. Translated into Russian it read:

'"On receipt of this you are to report to the Army Medical Directorate within two hours to await instructions . . ."

'This was a summons from that same gallant army, led by "Boss" Petlyura, which left corpses in the street and indulged in pogroms. And I, with a red cross armband, was to join that company.

'I did not waste much time day-dreaming on the staircase. I leaped up like a jack-in-the-box and went into my flat; this is where my suitcase came on the scene. I quickly worked out a plan: I would leave the flat, taking a change of underwear, and make my way to a *feldsher* friend of mine who lived on the outskirts, a man of doleful aspect and manifest Bolshevik sympathies. I would stay with him until Petlyura was thrown out, for there could be no doubt that he was going to be defeated. Or maybe the long-awaited Bolsheviks were a myth? Where were the guns? Silence had fallen. No, there was the rumbling again.

'I threw the shirt away angrily, snapped the lock of the suitcase, put an automatic and a spare magazine into my pocket, and donned my greatcoat with its red cross armband. Then I looked around miserably, put out the lamp and groped my way through the shadowy twilight into the hall. There I turned on the light, fastened the hood on to my greatcoat and opened the door to the landing.

'That instant I heard a cough, and two figures with short cavalry carbines slung over their shoulders stepped into my hall. One was wearing spurs, the other was not, and both had tall fur hats with blue tassels which dangled jauntily down to their cheeks.

'My heart missed a beat.

' "Are you Doctor Yashvin?" the first trooper asked in Ukrainian.

' "Yes, I am," I answered tonelessly.

' "You're coming with us," he said.

' "What's the meaning of this?" I asked, having somewhat recovered from the shock.

' "Sabotage, that's what," said the one with the loud spurs, and gave me a sly leer. "The doctors don't want to be mobilised, so they'll be punished according to the law."

'The hall light was switched off, the door clicked shut and we went down the stairs and out.

' "Where are you taking me?" I asked, stroking the cool ribbed butt of the automatic in my trouser pocket.

' "To the First Cavalry Regiment," answered the man with the spurs.

' "What for?"

' "Wha' you mean, what for?" The second man was surprised. "You've been appointed our doctor."

' "Who's in command of the regiment?"

' "Colonel Leshchenko," the first one answered with some pride, his spurs clinking rhythmically to my left.

' "What an idiot I was," I thought, "to waste so much time over my suitcase. All because of a pair of underpants . . . I could easily have left five minutes earlier."

'By the time we reached the house the city was covered by a black frosty sky studded with stars. A blaze of electric light shone through its large, ornate windows. With much clinking of spurs, I was led into an empty, dusty room, blindingly lit by a strong electric bulb under a cracked opal-glass lampshade. The muzzle of a machine-gun jutted out from a corner, and my attention was riveted by red and russet-coloured trickles on the wall by the machine-gun, where an expensive tapestry hung in shreds.

' "That's blood," I thought to myself and winced.

' "Colonel," the man with spurs said quietly, "we've found the doctor."

' "Is he a Yid?" barked a dry, hoarse voice.

'From behind the woven sheperdesses of the tapestry a door was silently thrown open and a man walked in. He was wearing a magnificent greatcoat and boots with spurs. A fine Caucasian belt decorated with silver medallions was tightly drawn around his waist, and at his hip a Caucasian sabre glinted in the bright electric light. He was wearing a lambskin hat with a magenta top crossed with gold braid. His slanting eyes had a cruel and curiously pained look, as though little black balls were bouncing up and down inside them. His face was riddled with pockmarks and his neat black moustache twitched nervously.

' "No, not a Yid," replied the trooper.

'Then the colonel strode up to me and looked into my eyes:

' "You're not a Yid," he began in a strong Ukrainian accent, speaking a horrible mixture of Russian and Ukrainian, "but you're no better than a Yid, and as soon as the fighting's over I shall have you court-martialled. You'll be shot for sabotage. Don't let him out of your sight," he told the trooper, "and give the doctor a horse."

'I stood there without saying a word, and as you can well imagine, the blood had drained from my face. Then once again everything started happening as though in a bad dream. A voice in the corner said plaintively:

' "Have mercy, sir . . ."

'I dimly perceived a quivering beard and a soldier's torn great-coat. Troopers' faces hovered around it.

' "A deserter?" croaked the now familiar hoarse voice. "God, you filthy wretch."

'I saw the colonel twitch at the mouth as he drew a grim, shining pistol from its holster and struck this broken man in the face with the butt. The man flung himself to one side, choking on his own blood as he fell to his knees. Tears poured from his eyes.

'Then the white, frostbound city vanished, a tree-lined road stretched along the bank of the still, dark waters of the mysterious Dnieper and the First Cavalry Regiment was marching along the road, strung out in a long winding file.

'At the rear of the column an intermittent rumbling came from the two-wheeled transport carts. Black lances bobbed along beside pointed hoods covered in hoar-frost. I was riding on a cold saddle, every now and then wriggling my aching toes in my boots. I breathed through a slit in my hood, which was growing a shaggy fringe of hoar-frost, and could feel my suitcase, tied to the pommel of the saddle, pressing against my left thigh. My inseparable escort rode silently beside me. Inwardly, I was as chilled as my feet. Now and then I raised my face to the sky and looked at the bright stars and in my ears, almost without cease, as though the sound had solidified, I could hear the shrieking of the deserter. Colonel Leshchenko had ordered him to be beaten with ramrods and they had beaten him in that house.

'The distant darkness was now silent and I reflected bitterly that the Bolsheviks had probably been beaten off. My fate was hopeless. We were making our way to Slobodka, where we were to halt and guard the bridge across the Dnieper. If the fighting should die down and I ceased to be of immediate use to him, Colonel Leshchenko would have me court-martialled. At this thought I felt petrified and cast a sad, longing glance at the stars. It was easy to guess at the verdict of a trial on a man who refused to report for duty within two hours in such a crisis. A horrible fate for a medical man.

'Two hours later the scene had again undergone a kaleidoscopic change. This time the dark road had vanished. I found myself in a room with plastered walls and a wooden table on which there was a lantern, a hunk of bread and the contents of a medical bag. My feet had thawed out and I was warm, thanks to the crimson flames dancing in a small black iron stove. From time to time cavalrymen came in to see me and I would treat them. Mostly they were cases of frostbite. They would take off their boots, unwrap their foot-cloths and crouch by the fire. The room stank of sour sweat, cheap tobacco and iodine. Occasionally my escort left me and I was alone. Always thinking of escape, I opened the door from time to time looked out and saw a staircase lit by a guttering wax candle, faces and rifles. The whole house was so packed with people that it was difficult to run away. I was in the middle of their headquarters. I would come back from the door to my table, sit wearily down, lay my head on my arms and listen attentively. I noticed that every five minutes according to my watch a scream came from the room below mine. By then I knew exactly what was going on. Someone was being beaten with ramrods. At times the scream turned into something like a lion's roar, sometimes into gentle, plaintive entreaties – or so it sounded through the floor – as though someone were having an intimate conversation with a close friend. Sometimes it stopped abruptly as if cut off with a knife.

' "What are you doing to them?" I asked one of Petlyura's men as he shivered and stretched his hands towards the fire. His bare foot was resting on a stool and I was smearing white ointment on the festering sore on his big toe, which was blue with cold. He answered:

' "We found an organisation in Slobodka. Communists and Yids. The colonel's interrogating them."

'I said nothing. When he went out, I muffled my ears in a scarf and the sounds grew fainter. I spent about a quarter of an hour like this, still haunted by the image of a pockmarked face under a gold-braided fur hat, until I was woken from my doze by the voice of my escort:

' "The colonel wants to see you."

'I stood up, unwound the scarf while the escort looked on in amazement, and followed the trooper. We went down the stairs to the floor below and I entered a white room, where I saw Colonel Leshchenko by the light of a lantern. He was naked to the waist and huddled on a stool, pressing a bloodstained piece of gauze to his chest. A helpless-looking peasant soldier stood by him, shuffling his feet and clinking his spurs.

' "The swine," the colonel hissed, and turned to me. "Come on, doctor, bandage me up. Out you go, lad," he said to the soldier, who clumped noisily out of the door. The house was silent. Then the windowframe shook. "Guns," I thought, shuddering, and asked:

' "How did it happen?"

' "With a pen knife," the colonel answered with a frown.

' "Who did it?"

' "None of your business," he retorted with a cold, spiteful malevolence, and added: "Ah, doctor, you're really in for trouble."

'Then it suddenly came to me: someone had been unable to endure his torture any longer, had made a rush for him and wounded him. That was the only way it could have happened.

' "Take off the gauze," I said and bent down to his chest with its thick growth of black hair. But before he had time to remove the blood-stained rag we heard footsteps outside the door, a scuffle, and then a coarse voice shouted:

' "Stop, stop, where the hell d'you think you're going?"

'The door was flung open and a dishevelled woman burst in. Her face was tensed in a way that made me think she was smiling; only much later did I realise that extreme anguish can express itself in very strange ways. A grey arm tried to grab the woman by her headscarf, but she tore herself free.

' "Go away, lad, go away," the colonel ordered, and the arm drew back.

'The woman stared at the half-naked colonel and said in a dry, tearless voice:

' "Why did you shoot my husband?"

' "Because he had to be shot, that's why," the colonel answered in his Ukrainian accent, grimacing with pain. The lump of gauze was getting redder and redder under his fingers.

'She gave such a smile that I could not help staring at her eyes. I had never seen such eyes. Then she turned to me and said:

' "And you're a doctor!"

'She poked her finger at the red cross on my sleeve and shook her head:

' "Oh, my God," she went on, her eyes blazing, "God, what a wretch you are . . . you trained at university and yet you can bring yourself to treat this murdering swine . . . tying nice little bandages for *them*! He thrashes a man in the face without cease, till he drives him mad . . . And you're bandaging him!"

'Everything blurred before my eyes and I felt sick; I knew that the most terrible episode in my wretched career as a doctor had begun.

' "Are you talking to me?" I asked, trembling. "Don't you know . . ."

'But she did not listen. She turned to the colonel and spat in his face. He jumped up and shouted:

' "Men!"

'They rushed in and he said in fury:

' "Give her twenty-five strokes with the ramrod."

'She said nothing as they dragged her out by the arms; the colonel closed the door and bolted it. Then he slumped on to the stool and threw away the ball of gauze. Blood trickled out of a small wound. The colonel wiped away the spittle that clung to his right moustache.

' "They're going to beat a *woman*?" I asked in a voice that I did not recognise.

'Anger flared in his eyes.

' "What?" he barked, looking at me with hatred. "Now I see what sort of a doctor I've been given!"

'I must have fired one of the bullets into his mouth because I remember him swaying on the stool and blood running out of his mouth; almost immediately it began to stream from his chest and stomach, then his eyes clouded and turned from dark to milky. Finally he slumped to the floor. As I pulled the trigger I remember being afraid of losing count and firing the seventh bullet, the last one. "That'll be for my own death," I said to myself. The smell of powder-smoke from the automatic was delicious. The door had barely started to crack before I hurled myself out of the window, breaking the glass with my feet. Fate was kind to me: I landed in an empty courtyard and ran past stacks of firewood into a back street. I would certainly have been caught if I had not run into a very narrow little blind alley between two walls; crouched on a pile of broken bricks, I waited in that cave-like space for several hours. I could hear cavalrymen galloping past me. The back street led down to the Dnieper, and they searched the river bank for a long time, looking for me. I could see one star through a crack – I think it must have been Mars. And then it seemed to explode: the first shell had burst, blotting out the stars. The night was filled with rumbling and crashing as I sat silent and motionless in my brick burrow, thinking about my degree and wondering whether the woman had died under the ramrods. When silence fell again, the dawn was just beginning to break and I came out of my hole, as I could not endure the torture of it any longer – both my legs were frostbitten. Slobodka was dead, everything was quiet, the stars had grown pale. When I reached the house it was as if there had never been a Colonel Leshchenko or a cavalry regiment. Only horse-dung on the trampled snow.

'I walked alone all the way back to Kiev, and when I reached the city it was broad daylight. I was met by an unfamiliar-looking patrol, wearing funny hats with earflaps. They stopped me and asked to see my papers. I said:

' "I am Doctor Yashvin. I am escaping from Petlyura's men. Where are they?"

'They told me:
' "They ran away during the night. A revolutionary committee has been set up in Kiev."
'I noticed one of the men of the patrol looking closely at me, then he shrugged sympathetically and said:
' "You can go home, doctor."
And off I went.'

After a pause I asked Yashvin:
'Did he die? Did you kill him or only wound him?'
Yashvin answered with his odd smile:
'Oh, don't worry – I killed him all right. Trust my experience as a surgeon.'